UPPSALA WOODS

UPPSALA WOODS

ÁLVARO COLOMER

Translated from the Spanish by
Jonathan Dunne

Hispabooks Publishing

Hispabooks Publishing, S. L.
Madrid, Spain
www.hispabooks.com

Originally published in Spain as *Los bosques de Upsala* by Alfaguara, 2009
First published in English by Hispabooks, 2013
English translation copyright © Jonathan Dunne
Design © simonpates - www.patesy.com

Cover image, Roots © Julie de Waroquier

A CIP record for this book is available from the British Library

978-84-941744-2-1 (trade paperback)
978-84-941744-3-8 (ebook)
Legal Deposit: M-25529-2013

I do not think about death at all,
but death thinks constantly about me.

THOMAS BERNHARD

Anyone who stays alive is always guilty.
But I shall bear the wound.

IMRE KERTÉSZ, *Liquidation*

There was once a wood in Viking Europe frequented by elders who had ceased to be of use to their community. These elders knew that Odin, also known as God of the Hanged, would only grant them entrance to the Great Banquet if they died in combat or if, having reached a critical age, they voluntarily took themselves out of the way. These men would enter the thicket, tie ropes to the branches and allow themselves to fall with the pride of someone who does not falter even before Death. The chronicles say that no one ever removed their bodies, and the hundreds of corpses there, all dangling a couple of inches above the ground, formed the most desolate—and poetic—landscape imaginable in the universe of suicide. We now know that this place, lost forever in the mists of time, was none other than Uppsala Woods.

1

I frequently curse the day I rented this apartment in the shape of a cross. Every evening, as soon as I return from work, I survey the corridor and recall the afternoon about a year ago when my wife informed me she had had enough of living in a place so linked with death as this. She then added that sometimes, having crossed the threshold of the house, she felt like starting to run, dropping her bag along the way and, having made it to the balcony, jumping over the railing, behind which was an abyss of seven floors. After hearing her confession, I dragged Elena to the office of a psychiatrist, who immediately diagnosed severe depression. A year has gone by since then, but I am still anxious that my wife might act out her fantasy. Which is why, when she doesn't come out to greet me shortly after hearing the door slam, I think about her suicide. I then shout, just as I'm shouting at this very moment, darling, I'm home, hoping she will appear from somewhere, almost always the living room, and show me she hasn't heard voices again that demand her presence from the confines of the precipice. But it so happens that tonight, after I've repeated that I'm home, nobody appears in a corridor growing narrower by the minute. I then survey the apartment. I contemplate the hallway leading to the living room, on the far side of which is the door to the balcony, the same door that a year ago beckoned to my wife, a door that is in fact a trapdoor to hell. Halfway from where I'm standing, intersecting the central hallway, there is another corridor, by the left of which one gains access to the bedroom and bathroom and, by the right, to the kitchen and my study. This, then, is a house in the shape of a cross. A dangerous house for any depressive. Dangerous for Elena. For the woman who today doesn't come out to greet me. She normally appears as soon as she hears my voice, asks me how my day has been and, having offered me her cheek so that I can kiss it, hangs my jacket in the closet. And yet today none of this happens. She doesn't cross the threshold of the living room, she doesn't say I'm coming, she doesn't show any signs of life. So I again declare that I'm home and wait for a reply. When it becomes obvious that nobody is going to answer, I imagine my wife is in the bathroom and decide to let her finish doing her things while amusing myself gazing at the door of the living room, a door that is unusually closed, a door behind which I sense all kinds of secrets. But I do not wish to let myself be carried away by negative thoughts. I mean that the balcony might have beckoned to Elena again, called her once more from the obscurity of night, invited her to take flight heedless of her apterous angel condition. I stay firmly where I am, downplaying the closed door, trying to convince myself that in a moment I will hear the toilet flush and she will appear from the left side of this crucifix in the shape of an apartment. At least this is what I long for. Because I couldn't bear any other situation, a more definite situation, so to speak, something like the final situation. Elena is my anchorage in this world, my small reality, my future. And I couldn't bear to lose her.

I repeat that I'm home because the wait is getting me down and, since I still don't receive an answer, I rub my hands together, not knowing what else to do. I doubt whether my wife would like me to hang up my jacket all by myself since she doesn't believe me capable of carrying out even such a simple operation as this. Elena says I always place the hangers back to front and, although it has been a long time since she was able to verify the truth of such a statement—basically because I haven't touched the closet since her last hysterical fit—I have no intention of contradicting her. What's more, for a year now, I have blindly followed all her orders, including the prohibition to approach a closet she devotes her many hours of spare time to. My wife has made this closet her last bastion of hope, as if tidying the closet stopped her thinking about other things, probably gloomier things, or as if ordering it helped her declutter her own head, which for some time now has been full of junk. For whatever reason, my wife spends the day lining up hangers, smoothing out shirts or combining colors, actions she carries out with greater frequency than is strictly necessary, proving once again that I live with an obsessive. Elena hangs up my jacket not only to make sure that the inside of this unit keeps the symmetries that so fascinate her, but also because over a period of months she has turned into a neat freak. Since she fell into a depression—and consequently lost her job—she spends the day cleaning the house and showing me how to perform household chores: how the shower curtains must always be drawn, how the knives must be put away with their cutting edge facing right, how the shampoo must never go in front of the shower gel, but behind it, how the shoes must point toward the wall, how the titles of books must be read from the bottom upward, and a wealth of other details that are impossible to recall if you're not as used to her as I am. In fact, the manual of prohibitions compiled by my wife is so thick that at this moment in time, whenever I prepare to undertake some kind of task, be it something ever so simple like doing the dishes, fluffing up the cushions or taking out the garbage, I'm afraid of making a mistake. To make matters worse, in the last few weeks, since the psychiatrist stopped the medication she was taking in the belief that she had got over the worst of her illness, my wife has introduced so many variations on the doctrines she herself created that I won't lift a finger without asking her first. And even so I make mistakes. I can be as still as a figure in a wax museum, I can undertake no action, I can even not be at home, but she still finds reasons for reproaching me and I, who have come across all sorts of different situations in five years of marriage, do not even protest. When she scolds me for something that truly doesn't make any sense, I simply tell myself that I don't care whether it has to be done in this or that way and, while apologizing for the supposed mistake or hanging my head in shame, I remind myself that I am still as very much in love with Elena as I was on the day I first met her. Or even more so. Only then do I stop feeling like shouting at her that, if she doesn't learn how to fight against these obsessions, she will end up tidying the pigeon-holes in a madhouse.

"I'm home," I insist.

A few seconds later, tired of standing at one end of the corridor, I move toward the other end in the hope of finding my wife in the living room, probably asleep on the sofa, the murmur of the television keeping time with her breathing. But on entering the living room, all I meet is the rattle of winter. Since my wife has left the balcony open in order to air the apartment, the cold of early March has invaded the room, and the wind-chill factor is so icy that even the lamp, swinging from side to side due to a gust of wind, seems to be shivering on the ceiling. Having checked there's no one outside, and stifling my urge to peer into the void to check Elena isn't lying squashed on the sidewalk, I close the door to the balcony and tell myself to stop imagining strange things. On turning around, ready to start exploring the rest of the apartment, I notice the handbag on the coffee table. My wife can't have gone anywhere without her set of keys, but there's no doubt she must have left the apartment because, as I proceed to verify, she's not in any of the other rooms either. I am still reflecting upon her possible whereabouts when it occurs to me, perhaps because I do not wish to entertain any other possibility, that she might be hiding somewhere in order to surprise me. After all, today is our wedding anniversary, and five years of marriage certainly deserve a bit of fun. Although I arrived home half an hour earlier than usual—since I wanted to take her out to dinner in the restaurant where I asked her to marry me— she could have heard the clank of the elevator and, having already decided a hiding place, slipped away before I came in. I imagine her right now crouching behind some piece of furniture, perhaps rubbing her legs so they don't fall asleep or suppressing a giggle with her hands, and can only feel glad that, after several months in a deep depression, she might have recovered the desire to behave like a little girl in a school playground. Before conducting a more thorough inspection of all the rooms, I wait a few seconds in the living room to give her time, in case it's necessary, to come out from under the table, shout happy wedding anniversary, darling, and fling her arms around my neck. But after a short while, when nobody appears from behind the tablecloth, I cross the threshold of the kitchen, whistling nonchalantly some kind of ditty, and, having spun around the thirteen square feet that constitute this hovel, I leave the place. I then head toward the bathroom, but I don't find her behind the shower curtain either, and the bedroom—the same bedroom where she barricaded herself during the first few months of her illness—and I sit on the bed, waiting for a hand to appear from beneath the base, grab one of my ankles and scare the living daylights out of me. I count to five in my head in order to give her time to frighten me—one, two, three, four—and, lifting the fifth finger, abandon the mattress in order to stand next to the closet, shout I'm going to lock it and wait again—one, two, three, four, five—for a reaction on her part. But my wife doesn't fling back the doors of the closet, she doesn't stretch an arm out from under the bed, nor does she even lift the lid of the trunk into which, in an act of contortion verging on impossible, she might have squeezed herself. And this is how I convince myself that only someone as

14

naive as me could possibly think that a woman who was so melancholic the day before might, from one day to the next, start behaving like a little girl in a school playground. I don't know how the idea of Elena preparing a surprise for me could have even crossed my mind when I'm perfectly aware that she detests any kind of celebration. Especially since she fell into that depression last year which, despite having been overcome by a combination of patience, therapy and drugs—most of all drugs—has left a touch of sadness in her character. I suppose the idea of a hiding place came to me because three weeks ago we went to a surprise birthday party organized by some friends for one of them, whom, to tell the truth, we hadn't called since his previous birthday. We accepted the invitation because the psychiatrist had recommended that we should get out more, have a social life to stop Elena's disorder returning with yet greater virulence, but neither of us particularly felt like spending even half an hour with people we stay in touch with purely out of politeness. Even so, we turned up at the event on time, and barely ten minutes had gone by since our arrival when I made an unforgivable mistake. While all of us guests were hiding in the birthday boy's bedroom waiting for him to come up, I remarked that no one had ever organized a surprise party for me. I said it as an anecdote, simply to keep the fifteen people squeezed into the room entertained, but I soon felt Elena's hurt gaze on me, as if she blamed herself for the fact that my friends had never crouched behind the sofa at home, waiting for me to appear, and immediately I regretted expressing my thoughts out loud. That same evening, as we were driving home, my wife apologized for being such a bore. It took me a few seconds to react since I didn't know what she was talking about, but I finally understood she was referring to the absence of a surprise party in my sentimental curriculum and I replied, perhaps a little too sharply, that she didn't strike me as being boring at all. I then added that I liked her just the way she was. The former was a lie; the latter, true. But she didn't believe either. She rested her head on the window, sulking in contempt, and informed me that she hated me being diplomatic even in love matters.

My wife isn't hiding under the bed, or behind the shower curtain, or anywhere else in this apartment, but she has left her bag on the coffee table, so the only place she can be is at the neighbor's house. The old woman who lives in apartment number two on the seventh floor has always got on well with Elena. But with me it's just the opposite. I remember shortly after we moved into this building, only a few days after our wedding, the widow started ringing at our door on a regular basis. In the beginning, she simply asked for help to carry out certain tasks she couldn't do herself on account of her age, such as changing a light bulb, shifting furniture or attending to the gas bottle delivery man, but after a few weeks her demands increased and included matters she was perfectly capable of doing, such as buying sugar, taking out the garbage or recording her electricity consumption on the corresponding sheet. For the first few months, I played along, aware that her real problem was not arthritis, but loneliness, and her requests disguised nothing but a desire for a bit of company. But at one point her interferences became so common it was impossible not to conclude that the only thing this woman couldn't do on account of her age was to leave us alone. And I wasn't wrong. In a short period of time, the woman had turned into a real nightmare. She would plant herself in front of our door at all hours of the day, always at the most inconvenient times, and wouldn't hide her satisfaction whenever, for example, she interrupted our dinner. She even gave the impression of being endowed with a sixth sense that enabled her to detect when her arrival would be most annoying. This busybody would ring the doorbell just as I collapsed on the sofa, got in the shower or sat on the toilet. Never when I was bored; always when I was relaxing. Needless to say, after a couple of months, I couldn't even lie down on the bed without being afraid she might appear. Once I even dreamed she sneaked into my bedroom at midnight, sat astride my belly and, oblivious to my warnings, repeatedly jabbed the nail of her little finger into my left eye. The following morning, still frightened by the widow's presence in my subconscious, I announced at home that I never again intended to help the Methuselah who lived opposite. Since then, my wife has taken on this role. She doesn't do it out of politeness, however, but out of friendship. Over the previous five years, and in particular during the last twelve months, they have become inseparable. So much so that I often doubt which of us is married to Elena. On top of everything else, whenever I've tried to explain the reasons why I despise the scarecrow next door, my partner has replied that my problem can only be designated with the word "jealousy". My wife believes I'm upset at being excluded from their intimate mutterings. But she's mistaken. What frightens me, what really frightens me in their relationship, is the possibility that the widow might infect my wife with her personality and I might wake up one day next to a person who spends so much time at home, the only fun she derives from life is snooping around other people's houses. That's what really horrifies me, not the other.

I wouldn't be surprised if tonight the neighbor had asked my wife for the help even her own children are not prepared to give her, in which case Elena might have left her bag on the table in the belief that I would be home from work before the end of her visit and so could answer the door when she felt it was time to come home. While I wait for this to happen, I sit on the sofa to bring myself up to date with the news on TV, but barely ten minutes have gone by when, in a state of anxiety as a result of the uncertainty of the current situation, I find myself ringing the widow's doorbell and crossing my fingers in the hope that the mystery surrounding Elena's disappearance might be cleared up once and for all. As I'm waiting for the neighbor to show the scouring pad life has given her in place of a head of hair, I suddenly feel someone's eyes on me, which makes me think that the old woman, instead of responding to my call, is observing me through the peephole. This woman always pretends she hasn't heard the tinkle of her own doorbell because she refuses openly to acknowledge that she spends all her waking hours sitting in the entrance hall of her home—obviously with her ear glued to the door and the cat on her lap—waiting for something to happen on the landing which, since she is so bored of herself, she has transformed into her own particular universe. There is no doubt that at this precise moment she is inspecting me through the peephole and in a short while, having finally emerged on to the landing, she will pretend that she has just crossed the corridor of her apartment with great suffering for her bones. And yet when after a couple of minutes the old woman deigns to open the door, she does something much worse than lie to me. She belittles me by asking me who I am. This human wreck knows perfectly well who I am, among other reasons because I have helped her on hundreds of occasions, but she throws this question at me to make it perfectly clear that she also feels a deep revulsion for me and to insist once again that I am not her cup of tea. When I identify myself as the neighbor who lives across the hall, she carries on feigning ignorance and doesn't even give in when I add that it's Julio, madam, Julio Garrido, from the seventh floor, apartment number one. When I perceive that even this explanation is not enough for her, I decide to bring this farce to a close by returning to my apartment. Needless to say, at precisely the moment I turn on my heels, the evil witch finally recognizes me and calls out my name, proceeding to open wide her front door so that I can fully appreciate the size of the entrance hall with which her flat begins. She does this out of pure malice, I am absolutely sure. I remember the day I met her—and therefore still didn't realize the extent of her wretchedness—I confessed that I was sorry to have rented an apartment without an entrance hall, and a moment later, without giving me time to finish my sentence, the old woman dragged me over to her own abode, where she showed me the magnificent vestibule with which the builder had endowed all the properties on the other side of the hall from mine. I have never understood what golden rule the architect applied in a building whose left wing residents should not enjoy the same privileges as those on the right, but the fact is that afternoon, as well as putting up with the stench of urine that emanated from her home, I found myself obliged to praise the virtues of an entrance hall I would have to cross on numerous occasions in the following months. After that first meeting, whenever I happen to meet the old bag on the landing, she opens the front door of her apartment as far as it will go in order to make sure that nothing prevents me from grasping the layout of her home and to make it perfectly clear that, while we both occupy houses in the worrying shape of a cross, hers is equipped with the most splendid pedestal. This woman's vileness, however, does not end there. On this occasion, after verifying that I am green with envy, she barks out that she hasn't seen Elena all day and proceeds to slam the door in such a way that it's a miracle she doesn't break my nose. I remain on the landing for a couple of seconds, stunned by the treatment I have received, and am just imagining myself setting fire to the front door of apartment number two on the seventh floor when it occurs to me that this crone, whose name I cannot even remember, has it in for me because my wife has told her too many details about our marriage and so she blames me for the depression Elena fell into a year ago.

Back at home, I no longer deny my innermost fears and muster enough courage to return to the balcony. There is no trace of Elena outside. My wife is not watering the plants, nor smoking a cigarette with her elbows on the railing, nor jumping out from behind the drying rack to give me the birthday surprise I dreamed of earlier. She simply isn't there. Next to the railing there is an easy chair, an ashtray full of cigarette butts and a pair of slippers neatly lined up against the bars. I am gazing at all these objects, sensing there must be a certain correlation between them—as if they bore witness to a series of events the pieces of which I shall only be able to fit together later—when I lean over the parapet and bow my head over the precipice. It is then, as I search for my wife's corpse on the tarmac, that I become truly afraid. I am behaving as if locating her body on the sidewalk would be the most natural thing in the world, as if death were a suitable hiding place for a surprise birthday party, or the great beyond the only destination one could go to without one's keys. I shudder at the idea. The fact of looking for her below reveals that deep down inside I still harbor the suspicion that Elena has not got over her depression and that her obsessions regarding household chores point to mental disorders of an alarming degree. The possibility that my wife has thrown herself off the balcony sparks off in me a dizzy spell I can only overcome by gasping for air, but the memory that today is our fifth wedding anniversary, together with the fact that she could have chosen this date, instead of any other day, to throw herself into the abyss, causes me to fall to my knees on the tiled floor, press my hands against the ground and vomit everything down to the last drop of bile. I am still racking my brains when I am reminded of our wedding day, when her mother whispered, possibly as a warning, that I should take great care of her daughter because, she added, fixing me with her eyes, Elena is a "crystal child". That's what she said. "A crystal child." At the time, I thought it was a simple metaphor, but with the passing of the years I have come to realize that she meant this advice to be taken seriously.

21

I had married an extraordinarily sensitive woman and for the rest of our lives would have to pay very careful attention if I didn't want her to shatter into a thousand pieces.

Although I glance over the railing a second time, I cannot make out the twisted shape of a body on the sidewalk, or a stretcher with a sheet covering the face of the deceased, or even a crowd pointing up at the firmament. I see none of this, perhaps because being so high up prevents me from detecting the tell-tale signs of a tragedy or else for the simple reason that there is nothing to be seen. And I don't know what to do. For a few seconds, I banish the ill omens by repeating that my wife would never commit such a foolish act as to allow herself to succumb to the voices of the precipice, and I go back to the sofa, sit down in front of the TV and concentrate on a newscast about a city devastated by a hurricane. While the anchorman gives a detailed account of the catastrophe, the cameras focus on a child walking over the rubble, on a woman holding a hairbrush and on an old man waving his hand at the viewers as if he didn't understand what had happened. At this point, I think that if my wife has taken her own life, I also will turn into a man waving at the audience with an expression of not understanding a thing. Barely a moment later, when I realize I've succumbed again to mortuary forebodings, I switch channels, anxious to lose sight of my peers' misfortunes. I want game shows where people win lots of money, comedy shows or advertisements oozing with happy scenes. Nothing depressing, only things that are upbeat. That's what I need. And yet, after swallowing an entertainment show for a little while, I soon realize that I'm still thinking about the abyss and it's not easy to forget something that has taken up abode inside your spirit. Especially when you have a trauma lodged inside your head. By which I mean what happened to me at the age of eight, when the woman who lived next door to my parents came out on to the balcony, placed a chair between two plant pots and, not caring whether I was playing on the adjoining balcony, launched herself into the void. She did this all of a sudden. First she was opposite the railing, then on top of the railing and, immediately after that, on the other side of the railing. Everything happened very quickly, without any big fuss. The neighbor had always treated me with great affection, but on that occasion she didn't stop to consider the impact her fall would have on me. She just kissed the crucifix hanging around her neck, glanced over at me and, with the tenderest of smiles, said see you later, Julito. Then she jumped. During the fall, I didn't take my eyes off that body which would end up crashing onto a mailbox, and yet I failed to understand what I'd seen until, from the fourth floor where we used to live, I glimpsed spaghetti spilling out of her nose. As she came into contact with the street furniture, the suicide's nasal septum produced some tasty-looking tomato noodles and, although it would take me several years to realize that these were the woman's fried brains, at the time I was convinced she had vomited up her lunch through her nose, which made me think that, if I decided to imitate her, I would inevitably have to sneeze up the pork chop and French fries I'd guzzled down a few minutes earlier.

When you have a trauma such as this implanted in your subconscious, a trauma that takes you back to the day when you froze on the balcony of your house without your mother realizing you were watching the next door lady's head bashed on the sidewalk—until a policeman pressed the intercom and started shouting for God's sake get that kid off the terrace—then, when a trauma such as this has infiltrated your brain and transformed itself into the essence of that very same brain, the only conclusion you can reach is that people have a tendency to leave your side without your understanding what it is that is so wrong about you that the whole world, your wife included, prefers death to being in your company. I spent half my childhood convinced that the lady next door had jumped for the sole reason that I was on the balcony. Not because she hated life or because she had problems at work, but because I was at her side, and for no other reason. I convinced myself that finding me there had made her sad enough to prevent her from smoking a cigarette leaning on the railing and decide instead to throw herself off into the abyss without thinking twice about it and, since my tender years did not allow me to rationalize the concept of someone taking their own life, I persuaded myself that, had I not been on the balcony at that moment, this woman would still be among us, which led me to think that my mere presence, in a way I found difficult to grasp, moved others to desolation. Over the years that followed this event, my parents went out of their way to get it into my head that the lady next door had jumped because she couldn't deal with the problems inherent in life, and not because she found me particularly unpleasant, but I only began to accept these justifications when I came to maturity, or rather after burying the memory in the underground tunnels of my subconscious. Until then, whenever I walked down the street, and in particular whenever I stopped next to a pedestrian crossing, I imagined the other pedestrians staring at me in horror and immediately throwing themselves under the wheels of a bus so they wouldn't have to put up with my company for a minute longer. Such images assailed my intellect with such frequency that I soon turned into an inward-looking child. Never looking outward; always looking deep into my own brain. And, needless to say, this trait in my character had a marked effect on my growing up and turned me into one of those kids who are always changing schools, resigned to the fact that, wherever they may be, and although there are no good reasons for it, they will always be the laughing stock of their classmates. Even many years later, when I enrolled in biology at the University, surely out of a fascination for the capacity of insects to form societies in which it wasn't the individual's character that mattered, but their usefulness, I never made friends, and it was Elena, no doubt drawn by my ability to withstand loneliness, who ended up showing me I also deserved a sprinkling of love.

But I'm letting myself be carried away by childish traumas that resurfaced in me when I found out that, from time to time, my wife imagines running down the corridor, dropping her bag and jumping over the railing. Such a realization caused me to think once more that I am such an unpleasant person that people will choose death over my company and, while I am now old enough to understand that this is just paranoia, I haven't been able to get rid of the thought for the past year. And yet now

25

is not the time to ponder such questions, but rather to focus on Elena's motives for harming her body. Which is to say on nothing at all. I say this not because a few weeks ago her psychiatrist claimed she had got over her depression, but because a woman like her would never commit such a foolish act. I consider my wife incapable of taking wrong decisions and, while she has recently been a little overwhelmed by the difficulties of returning to a job market she had to leave on account of her illness, I don't imagine her throwing in the towel either. In fact, her strength of character has always been an example for me. Even now, I recall the day when the doctor contacted me in order to explain the disorder that had plunged my spouse into such a pit of despair. For more than an hour, the physician discussed the details of her illness and the way I would have to behave from that moment onward, but I didn't listen closely to what he was saying because, at the start of our conversation, shortly after I'd sat down in his office, he blurted out a phrase that would buzz in my head for the rest of our meeting. He said that depression normally affected people with "an excessive mind", and I was so carried away by this statement that, instead of hanging on his every word, I got stuck on the idea of having married a woman with a higher than average IQ. Perhaps I shouldn't have confused the term "mind" with the concept of intelligence, but at that point in time I was so amazed that a person with an excessive brain could have chosen me, only me and nobody else but me, to spend the rest of her days with that I ignored any other consideration. That said, a year after this consultation, when the very same alienist diagnosed the end of her depression, I detected in Elena's character a touch of sadness that was possibly deeper than the melancholy that affected her the day I first met her. And yet the control therapies she was recently subjected to confirmed her recovery, and so I have ended up adapting myself to circumstances and accepting that, from now on, I will share my life with someone who, having developed a sudden tendency to get the blues, will never be the woman she once was. Fortunately, her bouts of depression do not affect her all that often, normally they happen when there's nothing on TV she likes, or when she notices she's just tidied the closet for the seventh time, or she suffers a setback in a job interview, the worst of which was when a businessman told her that, at the age of thirty-four and with no children, no one would be so stupid as to give her a job. That afternoon, Elena came home very depressed. She scolded me three times in the space of half an hour, but fortunately, after a few days, her pride recovered from this rebuff and, rising from the ashes, she opened the newspaper at the section of classified ads, underlined four job offers and declared that she would have one of these positions in a flash. Obviously, she didn't achieve this, but still today at breakfast, after having her usual coffee with milk and washing the cup before it even gets cold, she goes downstairs to buy several newspapers, the ads of which she pores over with relish. There are no motives therefore for her to harm herself, nor for me, in my determination to glimpse ghosts where there are barely any shadows, to become obsessed with this question.

Although my conjectures about her likely plunge persist inside my head, I avoid returning to the balcony, not wishing to foster such ill-advised ideas, and decide to kill time instead by walking around an apartment which, in addition to all my other traumas, reminds me now of the crucifix my childhood neighbor kissed before crashing against the mailbox. I wander down the corridor for a while, glancing constantly at my watch and rushing over to the peephole whenever I hear the clank of the elevator, and come to a halt in front of my study, gaze at the closed door and ponder that, when I thought my wife was hiding somewhere in the house, I didn't look in here. I didn't look in here because, as we agreed on the day we signed the contract and received the keys to the apartment, Elena never sets foot inside my work-space. Shortly before we climbed the stairs to the real estate agent's office, I asked my wife to let me convert this windowless room, which the architect undoubtedly had intended to be a kind of box room, into my private retreat, and she agreed almost without putting up any resistance. And yet, once we'd moved in and she'd begun to show the first signs of her obsessions, I understood that my wife had granted me this room on condition that I accepted that the rest of the house was hers. To begin with, I thought that she'd assumed that an individual like me—that is an individual who is always looking inward, and seldom outward—could only feel free if he owned a small room where he could withdraw to when he wanted to be alone, but it didn't take me long to realize that somebody like her—permanently aware of her own dominions and not at all prepared to allow interferences in the same—would only give up a room if she could get something out of it. And so, if she permitted me this tranche of freedom—what she, with a clear sense of irony, called the "creepy-crawly room"—it was because she knew that, from that moment onward, I would always talk about "her apartment", and not "our apartment", as a clear way of accepting her strange ideas on cohabitation. And proof of my ownership of this room is the fact that in here I can leave the drawers open, chuck my shoes in the corner and place a bottle of shampoo—needless to say in front of the gel—on the table without her saying a word. When I enter this broom closet, Elena doesn't disturb me and, in appreciation of this, whenever my wife tidies the living room for the third, fourth or fifth time, I do not bother her either. Besides, if my wife has an irascible day, one of those days when she gets annoyed over the slightest detail and tells me off for this, that or the other, I take refuge in the "creepy-crawly room", and there are no problems. I didn't inspect this room a moment ago since it struck me as inconceivable that she would break the rules of our unusual cohabitation, but now I open the door to my study in search of a clue to help me resolve the enigma of her absence, and the minute I set foot in the room I sense that my spouse has been rummaging through my things. I don't know how to explain it, but I have a feeling that she has spent quite a while in front of my desk, possibly tapping my microscope with the end of a pencil or perhaps examining the insect display case that adorns the only wall without bookshelves. Just as I am having this hunch I am assailed by the fear that she might have decided to throw herself off the balcony after spending long enough in my study for its limitations to sink into her soul. Because such a claustrophobic, as well as dark and gloomy, place would befuddle the mind of anyone.

Myself included. In spite of enjoying being enclosed in these four walls, being an inward-looking sort of guy, I realize that a ten square feet poky little room with no ventilation would drive the sanest person crazy. I try to banish such thoughts by observing the position of various objects in the light coming from the corridor, but I only manage to confirm that Elena was here when, next to the microscope, I discover her wedding ring. This makes me fly out of the study, bound across the living room and plant myself back on the terrace.

I survey the street carefully, paying particular attention to the pedestrians' gait in order to ascertain whether they are sidestepping a pool of blood impossible to make out from where I'm standing. But the light of the street lamps soon fills my sight with little spots, so I raise my head to relax my eyes and immediately come across a dog staring at me from the balcony opposite. I haven't seen this dog for a while. It belongs to the people of the seventh floor of the building on the other side of the street, they bought it four years ago. In winter, the owners of this flat keep the balcony closed to shield themselves from the cold, but the arrival of good weather causes them to open it and the dog, which must have been waiting for spring with elation, immediately emerges on to the terrace to spend hours, days, weeks even, with its head between the bars, its ears pricked and its eyes fixed on our home, something that would be beautiful were it not for the fact that it devotes itself to being a nuisance the moment it detects any activity in our living room. It barks non-stop at our window. It only needs the slightest movement to make a racket, sometimes not even that. In truth, there have been times

we weren't even in the living room or on the balcony—
and so logically it couldn't see us—and the howling went
on anyway. To begin with, I couldn't understand what
excited it so much if there was nobody in its field of vision,
but I soon suspected the scheming ways of the widow in
apartment two, imagining her pestering the dog from the
balcony next to ours and killing herself laughing at the
thought of me in bed unable to get to sleep. Fortunately
for her integrity, I have never caught her provoking the
mutt. And I would prefer not to. Because one of these days
when she least expects it and I find myself in possession of
sufficient proof of these and other dirty tricks, I shall stick
a knife in her door by way of warning. And then she will
stop bugging me with all her shenanigans, you bet she will.
That said, with the passing of the years, the dog's presence
has become unbearable not only on account of its growls,
but also because of its silences. I normally get angry when
I can't hear the television because of its barking, but last
summer, when my wife was going through the worst
period of her depression and as a result the atmosphere at
home was stifling, I was disturbed to realize that the dog,
instead of kicking up a fuss, was limiting itself to watching
us. As soon as I saw it outside, its head between the bars
and its tongue hanging out over the abyss, I was assailed
by the fear that my wife and I were spending too much
time ensconced on the sofa without interacting with each
other, disobeying the psychiatrist's orders about improving
our communication. I remember on several occasions,
when this Cerberus' quietude became unbearable, I myself
pretended I wanted a glass of water and abruptly stood
up, intending only to provoke a reaction on the part of

the animal. And while its barks banished any fear that our marriage might have turned into a hive of inactivity, I soon regretted having wound it up. The dog would get so excited there was then no way of getting it to shut up and, despite having knowingly caused it to lose its temper, I always ended up going on to the terrace to intimidate it with my stern look. Something I invariably failed to achieve, as you can imagine. The dog never drew back an inch in my presence, often rather the opposite, and only fell silent when its owner stuck a leg on the balcony to give it a kick up the ass. I would have preferred it to stop barking out of fear of my presence, but the neighbor always interfered in my psychological warfare with a well-directed kick. On my return to the sofa, however, I didn't let this prevent me from informing my wife that I had silenced the dog with my look. Reality was something totally different. I've never frightened anybody in my life. Neither dogs with a look, nor people with words. The last time I stood up to anyone was several months ago, when the neighbor on the other side of the street showed his face and I used this opportunity to shout from my balcony that I was utterly fed up with his dog's barking, but, instead of apologizing for the inconvenience caused, the neighbor contorted his face into a grimace of contempt, leaned over the railing and stared at me long enough to cause it to be me the one running away with my tail between my legs.

Tonight the dog is barking again and, being in the habit of placating the hatred that overwhelms me from time to time by fantasizing actions I would never dare carry out, I imagine placing my hand in my pocket, taking hold of my cellphone and, with a well-aimed throw, smashing its head with it. Although I lack the courage to turn this fantasy into reality, it makes me realize I haven't done something as elementary as phoning Elena up. I grab the phone, dial her number, and my chest starts getting tighter and tighter when I hear a tone coming from the kitchen, from the cupboard beneath the sink where we keep the garbage. I am hypnotized for several seconds by the sight of the cellphone's screen next to a banana skin beaming at me until I awake from my lethargy and hurry toward the exit, determined to go downstairs and search for any signs of a possible tragedy. I leave the house, stop in front of the elevator, press the button four, five, six times, grow impatient at the slowness of the contraption, gaze at the widow's front door, bite my nails, wait a few seconds more, start running down the stairs, jump three steps in a single go, dribble past a neighbor on the right, hear a crackling sound in my knee, trip over my left foot, wonder over and over again whether I'm overdoing it, notice the keys bouncing against my thigh, remember the lady next door who threw herself off the balcony of my childhood, feel my hand growing warm as a result of the friction with the banisters and, by the time I reach the second floor, where I pause to catch my breath, I am assailed by the image of Elena lying on the sofa at home. I don't know what causes me to evoke such an image at a time like this, but suddenly my head is full of identical scenes I find it impossible to dispel: my wife stretched out on the sofa, sitting on the left side of the sofa, reclining against the back of the sofa, hysterically punching the cushions on the sofa, brushing over and over the material of the sofa, and an endless barrage of situations with the sofa as their common factor. All the scenes involve the sofa and, try as I might to evoke different memories dealing with five years of marriage, all I get are those of the damn sofa. At this precise moment, having finally restarted my journey downstairs, I recall the day we purchased this piece of junk. It was on display in the shop where we had our wedding list and, while we lounged on top of its cushions to verify how soft it was, Elena leaned her head on my shoulders, gave a forceful sigh and assured me we would experience many hours of happiness on this sofa. And yet, on reaching the lobby and sticking my face outdoors, I realize that she hasn't known any happiness on this sofa. At the most she has been comfortable while on it. But that's all.

From my position in the street, I catch a glimpse of the dog's head sticking out between the seventh floor bars. Although there are other pedestrians near me, people coming and going, and others who stop, I could swear that the mutt is staring straight at me and, when I walk toward the right to check whether this is an optical illusion on account of the distance, I see the animal pricking up its ears, stretching its neck a little and pointing its snout in the same direction I'm going in. I have no idea how far a dog's eyesight can reach, but there is no doubt that this crazy mutt can discern my figure at a distance of eighty feet and that the widow next door, whom I also discover spying on me from her balcony, enjoys the same visual proficiency, because right now, when I wave to show her I've caught her, she takes a step backward and is swallowed up by the shadows of her terrace. A little later, once the busybody in apartment two has disappeared into the gloom of her loneliness and the dog on the other side has been kicked once again by its owner, I focus on the ground, greedily seeking a clue to confirm or refute my hypothesis. I search for a splash of blood, an odd earring or a pile of sawdust. Anything that will help me clarify whether or not Elena has pulped her brains on the sidewalk. But I find nothing at all. Not even a broken cobblestone. Needless to say, the other pedestrians stare at me in distrust because they're not used to finding men squatting in the middle of the road, and the occupant of a patrol car, clearly hankering after a bit of action, starts rubbing his hands in glee while driving past. This policeman's eyebrows are still raised when a teenager stops beside me, asks what I'm looking for and grows pale as I reply that it's none of her business. A couple of minutes later, having assured myself that the sidewalk is devoid of human remains, I look back up hoping Elena will appear on our balcony, shouting what are you doing there, you idiot, and ordering me to return home at once. And yet, since none of this happens and I cannot imagine anywhere else she might be, I have to accept that my wife has simply vanished without giving an explanation. She's not at home, she doesn't have her cellphone, she hasn't taken her keys, but since she hasn't crashed against the sidewalk either, the only other option is that she's fled as far away from me as she could. Elena has abandoned me because she can't put up with any more of my mistakes, because she's met someone else or because depression, if not insanity, has launched her into the world. Who knows? In spite of this, before allowing my thoughts to travel along such roads, I remind myself that I'm in the habit of blowing things out of all proportion and, as a final resort, I cling to the possibility of my wife still being at the job interview she told me during last night's dinner she had arranged for four o'clock this afternoon. Perhaps she has already passed the aptitude tests she's been taking all afternoon and now, when it's already past ten o'clock at night, she is being examined by a couple of pen-pushers intent on artificially extending the interview so that they can spend a little more time enjoying her talent and, indeed, her beauty. Encouraged by such arguments, I head home, prepared to wait in front of the television, but as the elevator glides past the different floors, I feel a growing distrust and, by the time I've reached the seventh floor, I'm beginning to think that Elena might have gone for a coffee with some of the girlfriends she stopped seeing as a result of her illness. Over the last year, she hasn't kept up with any of her acquaintances, with the sole exception of her brother, and these women haven't stopped phoning in an attempt to persuade her to come along to one of their outings by reminding her that, if she keeps her distance from the world, she will never regain the desire to live. It is possible that today, after hundreds of phone calls at ungodly hours and even the odd, ill-advised incursion into our home, this coven of meddlers has finally achieved its aim. I would rather this were not the case. I have never much liked all these busybodies. Mainly because they spend most of their time commenting on the unfavorable economic situation in which we live, not holding back when it comes to reminding my wife that they warned her about the consequences of marrying a man whose greatest ambition was to dissect insects. It makes my blood boil to think that on a day like this, our fifth wedding anniversary, when we should be having dinner in the restaurant where

I begged Elena to marry me, she could have re-established contact with that bevy of gossips, and the mere possibility angers me so much that no sooner have I set foot in our apartment than I head straight for the closet firmly decided to put my jacket on a hanger which, needless to say, I shall position back to front. I am still savoring the taste of revenge when, on opening the doors to this built-in closet, I find Elena lying inside. In the beginning I do not react. I gaze at her recumbent figure, but am unable to grasp the meaning of what's before me until I notice the bottle of barbiturates, the dried-up saliva and the eyes without pupils. It is then I curse the day when, hiding in a room with some other adults, I remarked that no one had ever organized a surprise party for me. Because this wasn't what I meant.

2

Barely ten minutes later, two paramedics knock at the
door of our house, say good evening and kneel down
next to my wife. At first, I have the impression they're
taking things far too easily, as if this wasn't an emergency,
but I soon understand that their unruffled attitude on
the job, as well as the rituality with which they lay out
all their instruments on the carpet, reveals a deep-seated
control of the situation, a habit even, a kind of mechanics
in the face of suicide. After that, when I've taken a few
steps back so as not to get in their way, one of them
asks why I didn't take the patient out of the closet and,
instead of replying straight away, I take a few seconds to
think about it. I am unwilling to admit I was terrified to
touch Elena's body, so I shrug my shoulders, trying to give
the impression that, like so many other urbanites, I am
paralyzed by other people's pain. A couple of months ago,
I witnessed a traffic accident in which a driver collided
with a motorcyclist. The impact sent the teenager flying
over the hood, causing him to turn two cartwheels in the
air and depositing him like a piece of twisted wire on top
of a manhole. A passer-by who just happened to be there
by chance immediately phoned for an ambulance while

several other bystanders reacted with the same alacrity and rushed to help the victim. These pedestrians reacted in a flash, as if they already knew what to do in such cases, while the rest of us stayed where we were, not daring to take part in a situation that was obviously too much for us. I myself stood paralyzed next to a traffic light, but after a while, just when a policeman started trying to revive the victim, I realized that I was no longer next to the traffic light, but behind it. While others had crowded around the injured person, no doubt fascinated by the fact that death could show its face in such an ordinary place, I had gradually concealed myself behind the traffic light without being aware of my actions, and still today I am surprised that my legs could have taken me away from the scene of the tragedy without having received, directly at least, an order from my brain. Tonight the same thing happened to me. Having found Elena lying inside the closet, I slid along the wall until I reached the phone and called emergency services, begging them to come at once, but then I remained in the corridor, my back pressed against the wall, my hands covering my face, unable to move out of fear. I didn't dare go back to the bedroom because I wasn't sure what to do in such a situation and, instead of behaving like the man that should exist somewhere inside me, I stayed in the corridor, pleading with God to spare my wife's life. Well, I didn't just plead for her life, I also asked for her not to realize that I'd left her on her own in what could turn out to be her final hour. My cowardice reached such levels that I preferred her immediate death over an agony that lasted long enough for her to perceive my abandonment. I was still tormenting myself about such moral baseness when I found myself squatting in a corner of the living room. Just as happened to me on the afternoon a motorcyclist perished on top of a manhole, I had moved from the corridor to the living room without realizing it, confirming that not only am I paralyzed by overpowering situations, but I'm also in the habit of removing myself from them unconsciously. For this reason, right now, as the paramedics are pulling Elena out of the closet and the neighbor's dog is barking on its balcony, I grasp the bedroom door, afraid that my legs might transport me to another room and horrified by the possibility that after a short while, when the doctors have finished what they're doing, they find me huddled behind the sofa cushions, curled up inside the trunk or sobbing next to an abyss of seven floors. I do not wish to abandon my wife in such circumstances, so I grab hold of the door frame while watching how one of the doctors injects a substance I suppose is adrenalin into the agonizing patient's arm and the other slaps her across the face a couple of times and orders her to wake up. After a moment, she suddenly obeys. My wife abruptly fixes her pupils on the man who has brought her back to life and, as he leans forward to welcome her literally to the paradise of second chances, she gives him a smile I wish could have been for me.

At this point, all I can do is repeat the words thank you while tears slide down my cheeks. One of the medical technicians puts away the instruments, ignoring my sobs, but his colleague, seeing me in such a predicament, pats me on the shoulder, assures me that everything will turn out OK and asks me to be a good boy and bring him a chair. I rush out of the bedroom, eager to be useful, and as I am heading toward the living room I hear them whispering behind my back. I don't mind. They can rant and rave about my cowardice as much as they like because, having resurrected my wife, they've also brought me back to life. Their insults do not offend me in the slightest, nor do I get upset when I return carrying the chair and they abruptly change the subject trying to pretend their whispers were just humorous comments concerning the patient's condition. They're trying to show me that the worst is over, that we should be glad because of my wife's recovery and we can even crack jokes at her expense, as one of them does by recommending that next time, if I don't have the courage to remove Elena from the closet, I should at least put a mothball in her pocket. They burst out laughing at this quip, but I don't. Nor do I protest. After all, they've given me back my wife and so I resign myself to their lack of tact and wait until one of them realizes I do not think this is the time for larking around and confirms that my spouse will get well. They place the patient on a chair which they drag toward the landing, where Elena, still drowsy, but equally beautiful, rests her head on the belly of one of her saviours and, although I would have preferred to see her reclining against my own bosom, I assume the role of stupefied husband I'm supposed to play. It is then I catch sight of the widow opposite peeping out from behind her door. The old lady appears on the landing as if by magic and gazes at my wife with such rapture she seems on the verge of embracing her at any moment. Fortunately, she just asks what is going on, and one of the paramedics, on seeing that I'm not going to reply, answers it's nothing, madam, go back inside, and don't worry. But the woman insists. She interrogates us about Elena two, three, four times, and is such a pain in the neck that the other paramedic, who is also surprised by my silence, informs her that the patient is suffering from a common case of indigestion. Of course, she doesn't buy this. Nor does she hide her indignation when she realizes she's being treated like a senile old bag. She is suddenly filled with hostility toward my person and, pointing her false nail at me, she shouts that I'm to blame for everything. In the seconds that follow, the landing is immersed in complete silence. That is until my wife places a hand on her savior's chest and a loud cry rises up from the cavern of her throat, causing me with her reaction to awake from my lethargy and order the widow to shut the fuck up. At which point I push the paramedics into the elevator and, telling them I'll use the stairs, I send them down to the ground floor. Once I am finally left alone with the old witch, once there are no longer any witnesses in the vicinity, once the world seems to have been reduced to just this landing, I take a step forward, draw myself up to my full height at a couple of inches from where she is and clench my fists with such force that even the hairs of her cat stand on end. I can smell the stench of urine coming from the old woman's dressing gown, but even more clearly I sense how her soul reeks of fear, and this odor fills me with courage, turns me into pure aggressiveness, gives me power, such overwhelming power I have only to suggest to this old wreck that she vanish from my sight for her to take several steps back, enter her hall and, merging with the shadows of her apartment, close the door without saying a word.

When I reach the street, one of the paramedics tells me to get in the ambulance as quickly as possible, and I have just started running when, in front of the lobby, all on its own on the cobblestones, looking absurd in such surroundings, I catch sight of the chair they have used to carry Elena downstairs. My wife would never forgive me for abandoning this seat to its fate. What's more, I am quite sure that, on her return, she will kick up a fuss not only because I left this piece of furniture out in the open, but because I went out without having first tidied the closet, even if, let it be said in passing, she herself disarranged the hangers when she had the bright idea of hiding inside it. But I mustn't waste time on such matters now, so I get in the back of the ambulance and fall flat on my face on top of the bench as the driver presses down on the accelerator. I gaze at the chair through the cracks and, seeing it there, in the middle of the sidewalk, as if waiting for someone to use it, I am overcome by the same sense of loneliness I experienced as a child that afternoon when, having witnessed my neighbor's fall and the spaghetti spilling out of her nose, I saw her husband emerge on to the selfsame terrace, survey the selfsame void and, having caught sight of the cadaver sprawled across the mailbox, mount the selfsame chair his wife had used as a trampoline a little earlier. The man remained there for quite some time, I suppose plucking up courage to emulate his spouse's flight, but in the end he got off the stool, huddled in a corner of the balcony and, still without noticing my presence, burst out crying. Since then, whenever wanting graphically to represent the concept of solitude, I am assailed by the image of a man weeping next to an empty chair. It is precisely this image that takes control of my brain as I stare at the seat abandoned in front of the building and feel the same uneasiness I experienced on that terrace in the past, an uneasiness that would make me weep were it not for the paramedic beside me. This man pays no attention to the patient, but focuses instead on the artificial respirator, the serum bag and the contraption with the vital signs. Not on my wife. I am still observing how this individual can be so absorbed by the gadgets crisscrossing Elena's body when he returns my gaze. At this point, he looks angry. Fed up perhaps. Possibly tired. He may have already witnessed the death of a couple of people on the stretcher where the patient is resting, and this is why he screws up his face, or it could be that he blames me for the situation my wife is in and wants to show me his rejection by scowling in this fashion. Whatever the reason, his attitude puts so much pressure on my conscience that, afraid he might really consider me responsible for the current circumstances, I swear that it wasn't my fault. I say this in a whisper, as if talking to myself, and the paramedic, undoubtedly used to all kinds of reactions on the part of those who accompany victims in the ambulance, merely rests the crown of his head against the window, fixes his eyes on the ceiling and sighs in resignation. Immediately after that, more concerned about earning the paramedic's respect than about caring for my wife, I take Elena's hand, smooth her hair and mutter I'm here darling, at your side. I know the orderly approves of what I'm doing because the patient is in need of human contact, but we're both aware that there's something artificial in my actions and I'm stroking her fingers because I have to, not because

I really want to. The problem is at that very moment I feel a deep sense of rejection toward my wife, toward her act, toward this attempted desertion perpetrated by the woman who swore to be with me for richer, for poorer, in sickness and in health, and in I don't know what else and what not. I behave with tenderness because I understand she needs my support, but the truth is I feel a strong desire to jump out of the ambulance and run off in any direction, perhaps toward the beach, possibly toward the city limits, maybe toward the land where deserted husbands go. Instead of this, I bend over Elena's body in order to kiss her on the forehead, since the artificial respirator prevents me from doing so on her mouth, and, just as I'm bringing my face closer to hers, the ambulance abruptly brakes, the paramedic leaps off the bench, flings open the back door, jumps on to the tarmac, pulls out the stretcher, lets out a cry, gestures at someone, greets a doctor, remarks he has a case of barbiturate intoxication, delivers some papers and hands over to a porter who pushes the stretcher toward the psychiatric emergency ward of the hospital we have arrived at. A moment later, when Elena has disappeared behind the automatic doors and I'm supposed to be running after her, I stop in front of the paramedic because I feel obliged to thank him for his efforts. The guy is standing a couple of feet away, waiting for me to speak, and all I can say, having never felt so judged in all my life, is that today is our fifth wedding anniversary. At which point the man pats my face, points to the entrance to the building and again asks me to be a good boy and wait in the waiting room. He then gets in the ambulance, jots something down in a file and gives me a sidelong glance.

After the vehicle has disappeared around the corner and I find myself alone in the middle of the parking lot, I am overwhelmed by the same sense of loneliness that took hold of me when I observed the abandoned chair in front of our building or when, many years earlier, I spied on the husband who found it impossible to follow his wife into the beyond.

Inside the psychiatric emergency ward, there is an atmosphere of absolute calm. To the right of the lobby there is a sitting area with a group of people waiting for news of their relatives; to the left is a counter with a nurse talking on the phone; and opposite there is a row of securely fastened doors, just in case some paranoiac should decide to escape at the least expected moment, behind which the newcomers are seen. I head over to the receptionist in order to ascertain where my wife is, but before I can say a word, the woman raises a finger, asking me to wait until she finishes her conversation. A few seconds later, I identify myself as Elena Domingo's husband, but then stop mid-sentence as I'm about to mention the reason for which my wife has been admitted. My lips remain sealed as soon as I attempt to pronounce the term that defines the act perpetrated by the patient and, although I imagine a psychopathological ward is not exactly the place for observing niceties, only now I realize I'm ashamed to admit openly that my wife has grown tired of living. I remember during my adolescence everybody made fun of the woman next door's husband because, a couple of years after he'd been widowed, and so when nobody cared any more about what had happened, he continued affirming that his wife had slipped while watering the plants.

Although all the other residents knew perfectly well the whole story, among other reasons because my mother had taken it upon herself to communicate to all and sundry my own version of events, this individual carried on trying to persuade us that her death had been the result of the most stupid accident, and, tired of putting up with all his fantasies, people used to reply of course, Manolo, your wife slipped while handling the plant pots hanging from the balcony ceiling. Detecting a certain amount of sarcasm in their comments, the widower reasserted his theory that she had tripped and did so with such perseverance that, as far as I can remember, people avoided talking to him just so he wouldn't annoy them repeating over and over something they weren't interested in. In fact, the man was so determined to swear that black was white that, on one occasion, the boy from apartment two on the third floor, a particularly troublesome child, shouted at him to stop banging on about his deceased wife because we all knew she'd thrown herself off the balcony in order to lose sight of him and, at the same time, to fuck up poor Julito's life. Needless to say, after such a blow, the widower suffered a turn, and he woke up a couple of hours later without remembering anything that had happened, at least so he affirmed, because over the following years whenever he had the opportunity Manolo carried on defending the theory that she had stumbled and only gave up on his insistence to transmute the facts one evening around the middle of May, if my memory doesn't fail me, when the two of us coincided in the elevator. My mother had warned me not to talk to our neighbor under any circumstances, and so I always looked through the peephole before going out on to the landing and sometimes, when I saw him in the vicinity of the building, I would hide around a corner while waiting for him to leave. But one evening I ran into the entrance hall, needing to do a wee, and careered into the elevator without noticing the person who had just got in, and, on bumping into the widower multiplied a thousand times by all the mirrors, I didn't dare effect a retreat. Barely had we embarked on our journey up to the same floor when the widower kneeled down in front of me, placed his hands on my shoulders and burst into tears while asking me to forgive him through a mixture of snot, trembles and whines. I didn't know what to do. Except to press my back against the wall and pee in my pants. Fortunately, we lived on the fourth floor, so I was able to escape fairly quickly, leaving this man, who in theory had to get off at the same floor, in an elevator immediately required by someone else, who must have been quite shocked on finding the crazy widower on his knees inside this empty, pee-stained vehicle. I remember all of this now because I also feel incapable of pronouncing the word that defines my wife's course of action and because I am somehow afraid that I will end up transfiguring reality in the same way this man did during my childhood. And yet, when I finally manage to brush away these memories from my mind, I discover the receptionist gazing at me with certain indifference. My state of absorption has not surprised her basically because she works on a psychiatric emergency ward, which has made her immune to the strange behavior of human beings, and also because she has a file with all the names of the new arrivals, as well as the reasons for their admission. So, having glanced at

Elena Domingo's admission form, she gives me a deeply compassionate smile, suggests I take a seat until I hear my name and, in the same tone used by the paramedic when he welcomed my wife to the paradise of second chances, she whispers to me that everything will be all right.

I sit down next to a man who, as I approach, bows his head, stretches out his hand and wishes me good evening. I reply to his greeting out of politeness, but immediately lean the other way, because I have no wish to engage in conversation with anyone. In spite of my clearly introverted behavior, this man continues staring at me as if he didn't realize he was being ignored, and, afraid that he might try to ask me the reason for my visit—something I have no desire to talk about—I decide to invent a lie—for example, Elena has suffered an anxiety attack—to avoid having to give further explanations. Fortunately, the minutes go by without the man attempting to initiate any dialogue and, when I look again, I discover he's reading the newspaper as if nothing has happened. I proceed to survey the gathering with curiosity, perhaps searching for nutcases amongst us, but everybody is behaving quite normally, as if waiting to visit the dentist instead of the booths of a psychiatric ward. I am even more surprised when a woman sitting a few rows in front of me is summoned by the loudspeaker and she gets up immediately, walks over to the receptionist's counter and gulps down the pills she's been given. It's now I realize I'm not surrounded by the patients' relatives, but by the patients themselves. My city's fellow lunatics are calmly sitting in this waiting room because contemporary medicine no longer treats the insane, but normal people, people like my wife or me, inhabited by monsters impossible to describe. I'd imagined that the emergency section of a psychiatric hospital would be full of loonies swinging to and fro, dribbling on their clothes or holding forth with invisible entities, but I only have to look around to understand I'm in a building with people so medicated, so perfectly medicated, they do not even look mentally ill. This worries me even more. Especially now, as I give a sidelong glance at the man who greeted me a moment ago or at the woman biting her nails a few rows behind me, when it occurs to me the lunatics of this century appear sane and every morning, when I leave the house to go to work, I walk alongside a bunch of nutcases who, although they give the impression of being serene, could at any moment adopt a different attitude. I've never stopped to think that the concealment of madness is a sign of our times and, judging by the peaceful atmosphere in this waiting room, I cannot help wondering how many people I know are taking medication secretly because they fear to admit openly that life, that fast track life we all lead, has become unbearable. A while ago, I read in a magazine that anti-depressants were the best-selling drug in this country, there were even statistics one in three citizens would suffer some kind of mental disorder during their lives, but I never stopped to consider the significance of such statements until now, when I am surrounded by ordinary-looking people who, however, have to visit a psychiatric emergency ward—not a psychiatric ward, but a psychiatric emergency ward—on account of some switch going off inside their heads. And despite being overwhelmed by such thoughts, mainly because they make me question the social model in which we are all installed,

I take comfort from the idea that, if one in three citizens is due to suffer some kind of mental disorder during their lives, I can consider myself free of such illnesses because I already went through my period of instability when I was a boy, by which I mean after I witnessed the suicide of the woman next door, a circumstance that not only turned me into a child who always looked inward, and never outward, but also into a young man with serious problems of integration. I remember now all those afternoons at school when, surrounded by classmates who never failed to treat me with utter cruelty and wouldn't stand the attacks of incontinence I suffered from until the age of fifteen, I would get up from my desk to ask the teacher for permission to go and change my underpants because at the time I urinated anywhere for no particular reason, unless one were to take into account the trauma lodged inside my brain. On such occasions, I would remain standing in the center of the room, waiting for the teacher to realize my trousers were wet, and I only dared to move when the teacher in charge that day adopted her usual expression of disgust and said for Heaven's sake, Mr. Garrido, get out of here immediately. And since these teachers, who were almost always women, never displayed even an iota of compassion toward the boy suffering from enuresis—their behavior was rather the opposite—I am now afraid that the receptionist, who in my imagination is a copy of the teacher who was so disgusted about my urine, will not let me leave the sitting area where I am at present, so I slowly stand up and wait for her to grant me permission to distance myself from all these normal-looking loonies. Then, when the receptionist notices me standing in the middle of the room, staring at her with my shoulders turned toward the exit, she winks at me as if to say that in this hospital, and in the adult world in general, I can do whatever I like without having to seek anyone's approval, and suddenly I feel happy to be in a place where people with problems get help, and not in a school where emotionally underdeveloped children are made fun of. Before abandoning my place, I glance around, taking comfort from the idea that on this occasion the weirdoes are the others, not me, and for a couple of seconds I am so pleased by my psychic stability that I gaze at the group with a sneer of superiority which threatens for a moment to turn into a large guffaw, something that would undoubtedly have happened had it not been for the fact the loudspeaker has suddenly mentioned my name, reminding me that I am here because my wife has tried to take her own life, a state of affairs so opposed to my urge to laugh that I end up gazing at all the patients in the room, thinking that all of us, every single one of us, are condemned to enter the dark tunnel of mental illness. And this is no laughing matter.

Barely a minute later, when I've approached the counter to point out that I am the Julio Garrido who has been summoned over the loudspeaker, a doctor appears and, looking up from the folder in his hands, asks me to follow him. We enter an office where there is only one table, three chairs and an empty bookshelf, a setting as austere as the doctor in front of me, with a face so expressionless it provokes rejection. In fact, you could say that somebody has erased his features with a rubber or, worse still, that he himself has scraped them off so nobody will guess the kind of thoughts circulating inside his brain—no doubt sinister thoughts—whenever a patient tells him something crazy. When I gaze at the buttons he seems to have in place of eyes, and the zip he's been given as a mouth, the guy remains immutable in his chair. He doesn't smile, doesn't talk, doesn't blink. One might say he doesn't even breathe. He just watches me in the utmost silence and nods from time to time, as if agreeing with himself, or as if the hand controlling the strings of this medical puppet suffered occasional spasms. Needless to say, I find his attitude extremely annoying. Every time he displays conformity with some deduction that seems to have arisen inside his noggin, I feel like laying into the sack genetics has placed on top of his shoulders, but manage to stifle my aggressiveness while waiting in the chair for this marionette finally to open his mouth.

"Are you aware of the fact that your wife has tried to commit suicide?" he blurts out.

I do not reply because, on hearing the noun that defines the act perpetrated by my spouse, which this alienist has mentioned with absolute impunity, something goes boom inside my head. I never thought a simple word could trigger such suffering in my soul, but the term sears my spirit so strongly I think I may suffer the same kind of fit experienced by the neighbor of my childhood when the boy from apartment number two on the third floor shouted that his wife hadn't tripped while watering the plants, but had jumped in order to lose sight of him and, at the same time, to fuck up poor Julito's life.

"Is this the first time she has tried to commit suicide?" he continues.

On this occasion, despite the fact that I nod very obviously, the doctor ignores my response and, leaning over his desk, qualifies the question:

"Are you sure, absolutely sure, this is the first time the patient has tried to commit suicide?"

Until a moment ago, I was sure, absolutely sure, that Elena had never perpetrated such an act as she did this evening, but now, finding myself in front of a psychiatrist who has examined hundreds of similar cases, I'm no longer so sure. When you think about it, anyone could have raised a hand against themselves without anyone else knowing about it. The doctor in front of me, for example. This man may well occupy his evenings composing the word "death" with pills he steals from the hospital and, after spending several hours gazing at the word, he might unzip his lips and swallow the "d", the "e", the "a" and so on. And perhaps after a while, having stretched out on the sofa to wait for this same term to re-form inside his stomach, he drags himself to the toilet because fear, only fear and nothing else but fear, forces him to vomit even the slightest bit of the word he has ingested. In the same way, the neighbor of my childhood could have tried her luck on other occasions, but only dared to jump over the railing when she was convinced she had a witness and so her act would last in somebody's memory. As a result, I am not in a position to state that Elena hasn't made this attempt in the past, or that over the preceding week she hasn't been trying out other hiding places before deciding on the closet, or else that now, while the doctor wastes his time playing guessing games about my wife's secret activities, she isn't slashing her wrists with some scalpel from the hospital. And since I'm unable to confirm any of these things, I prefer not to reply to a question that was clearly rhetorical, designed to fill me with doubt. This doctor has interrogated me twice on the same subject because he wants me to understand that nobody, absolutely nobody, is free of suspicion and now, as he shows his satisfaction with the unease provoked in me by his questions, he makes himself comfortable, he passes his hand over his mouth and rests his head against the back of his chair.

"Your wife will come out of this," he goes on, "but you have to understand there's a good chance she will try again. Statistics show that almost all failed suicides repeat their attempt within ten years."

It upsets me to hear him using the term "failed", as I believe he shouldn't refer like that to people who didn't manage to die.

"This means that for the next ten years you're going to have to be on the lookout for any strange behavior on the part of the patient."

Ten years, whispers a voice inside me. Ten, it repeats.

"My wife has just gotten over a depression," I blurt out in the hope that this information will somehow prove useful.

"Yes, well, that is logical," he mutters and, without giving my remark any importance, he continues, "We will now begin a treatment in order to help your wife. With a bit of luck, we will find out she is still suffering from a simple mental disorder, and …"

"A simple mental disorder?"

The tone with which I ask this question strikes the psychiatrist as insolent, and he straightens his back a little in order to make clear who's boss in this office.

"Ninety-five percent of suicides are suffering from some kind of mental disorder which can be cured using psychotropic drugs and therapy."

"What about the others?"

"What others?"

"The other five percent."

"That percentage corresponds to suicides who adduce philosophical causes. But I don't think your wife is one of those."

"Why not?"

The doctor seems to hesitate:

"Let's just say it's not easy to find people who give up life as a result of existential arguments. Most failed suicides who come to us are suffering from some serious mental disorder. And the fact is, Mr. Garrido, I don't think this case is going to be any different."

Even though it's abundantly clear that this doctor has never come across a patient prepared to abandon life for more noble reasons than a simple neuronal disorder, and even though there is also no doubt that his faith in science would prevent him from recognizing such a case even if it hit him on the nose, I remain convinced that my wife belongs to the five percent of people capable of endowing their death with philosophical meaning. And yet I lack the evidence to certify my wife's superior intelligence and so I stay quiet before a specialist who doesn't believe in five percent of soul motivations basically because he has only ever encountered ninety-five percent of body casuistries and is therefore so used to imbalances in the chemical make-up of the brain that he wouldn't be able to diagnose a case of existential angst even if the individual in question had used the encyclopedia of pessimism as a stool to stand on before placing his head inside a noose. Right now, as I contemplate this man's featureless face and verify that the buttons of his eyes do not emit the slightest glimmer of humanity, I am sure he will never discover other symptoms in his patients than those strictly related to serotonin. And only those. No humanism, atheism or any other current of thought. Just a breakdown in the neurotransmitter, nothing else. He even seems to believe that the other five percent that don't match the statistics are caused by some kind of brain condition science has yet to discover, but will be explained as soon as technology permits, at which point voluntary death will be such a purely biological act it won't even be worth weeping over any human being who had every intention of turning into a corpse.

"How can I stop this happening again?"

"We get to suicide by learning," he replies, making out he has a suitable phrase for every occasion. "Your wife ingested a whole blister pack of sleeping pills and didn't die. She has now learned that one pack is not enough, so next time she will try two. If she fails again, she will triple the dose. Then quadruple it. And then, Mr. Garrido, then, she will die. Mistakes teach us, which is why I say we get to suicide by learning."

I want to ask him a second time what I must do to prevent my wife from harming herself because I have the impression he hasn't answered my question, but the doctor anticipates my desire showing, by doing so, how those in his profession are always one step ahead:

"From now on, you must talk to her. Talk to her two or three times as much as you used to. You have to understand that a suicidal person's anxiety only calms down when they verbalize the thoughts inside their head. Silence makes people fantasize, Mr. Garrido, and in suicidal matters fantasizing is the worst possible thing. After moments like this, we always recommend that relatives do not hold back when it comes to discussing death, we advise them to talk openly about it. This is the only way to stop your wife from trying again. I repeat: the only way. But, if it doesn't work, then you must spy on her. Keep a constant eye on her moods and, whenever she appears sad or even when she appears overjoyed, be suspicious. Mood swings are indicative of some kind of disorder, but sudden periods of calm, even more so. If your wife is usually on edge and suddenly appears calm, then something's up. She may have calmed down because she's taken a decision, a decision you are not going to like. Many potential suicides enter a period of absolute tranquility right before they raise a hand against themselves. This is because they've planned their own death so carefully they no longer see themselves as part of this world. They find this soothing. So your mission from now on is to watch for any changes in your wife's mood. Never stop being suspicious, Mr. Garrido, because suspicion leads to anticipation."

He examines me carefully to see if I have followed his explanation and then proceeds:

"Bear in mind almost all suicides leave clues about their intentions. But you have to be able to spot these clues. Any detail, however insignificant, may conceal a warning. Any detail, understand? Any."

"But why does she want to die?"

The doctor rubs his forehead, as if he himself has spent years trying to figure out the correct answer to that question, and explains:

"The idea of suicide is physiological. There comes a time when certain people begin to experience a pain that prevents them from living and, when asked about the origin of this pain, they reply that it comes from life itself. As if life itself were the illness, understand? For such people, life is pure pain. Not long ago, a patient told me that every morning he feels he's being tied to a rack from which he is not released until it is time to go to sleep. As he explained it, the rack caused him a general pain that didn't affect one organ in particular, but somehow damaged them all. A pain you and I would refer to as pain in the soul because we have no other way of describing it, but which he defined as physical pain. Obviously, this man was talking about a pain no scanner would ever pick up for the simple reason it's being generated in the most enigmatic part of the human body …" At this point the doctor taps one of his temples. "If you felt such pain every morning, every morning of the week, every week of the month, every month of the year, in the end you would wish for there to be no more mornings. I know it's not easy to understand, but all suicides we've been able to interview claim, using different words, that life causes them unspeakable pain. And they're not talking about an abstract kind of pain, Mr. Garrido, but a very concrete one."

He waits for me to stop squirming in my seat before continuing:

"So far, psychiatry hasn't found a common denominator among people who refer to this sort of pain. There are certain markers which crop up in the majority of cases—a drop in the level of a particular neurotransmitter, environmental conditions or family history—but none of these indicators is defining. In other words, there are currently no determinant factors to explain why some people want to live and others want to die. And yet, even though we cannot say why it happens, we are able to fight it. Pharmacology has advanced a great deal, Mr. Garrido. We have already managed to make ninety percent of patients with neuronal disorders recover the will to live in a couple of months. Now that is a real step forward."

"But why has this happened to my wife?"

"Chance," says the doctor, pretending he doesn't mind openly admitting that science hasn't achieved a more empirical answer to my question. "We would have to analyze your wife's particular case, but probably wouldn't find any motives which on their own would explain why she tried. The desire to commit suicide is like depression, schizophrenia or even blindness: it can happen to anyone."

I feel extremely relieved there are no decorative objects in this office because the discovery that psychiatry believes Elena's brain has become distorted as a result of pure chance, and not for any more elevated reason, makes me want to grab a sculpture and smash it on the gourd of this dummy dressed up as a psychiatrist.

"From now on, whenever your wife thinks about death, you must convince her to wait another day before doing something terrible," he continues. "I know it is difficult to comprehend, but all failed suicides, absolutely all, say that the idea of committing suicide appeared in their heads suddenly and they simply decided to carry it out. The idea of committing suicide, the idea in itself, is impulsive. It appears out of the blue and, wham-bam, they kill themselves. Which doesn't mean these people hadn't already thought about taking their own life. Quite the opposite. They had thought about it a lot, an awful lot, but the act itself, the materialization of the thought, is sudden. They abruptly reach the conclusion that today is a good day for doing something they've pondered so much, and they do it."

The doctor falls silent for a moment, probably because he's musing over his line of thought, and then goes on:

"Even though they've considered the possibility of dying on other occasions, they only put it into practice when the idea turns into an imposition, into a voice that shouts, "Stop thinking about it and just do it!" The following morning, assuming they have survived, all of them, without exception, regret having tried. Do you understand what I'm saying? Nobody—and I repeat, nobody—can be suicidal twenty-four hours a day. If you manage to persuade your wife not to take her own life today, she probably won't want to try again tomorrow. She might think about it again after a week, but five years may pass before the order reappears inside her brain. Or it may never do so. Which is why you must keep an eye on her mood and at the slightest change—the slightest, I tell you—convince her to wait another day. If she doesn't seem willing to listen to you, insist. Tell her time and time again that she can always commit suicide tomorrow. This is the most effective sentence that exists. Tell her to wait another day, and you'll see how the following day she no longer wants to die. After all, the idea of suicide competes with one of the most basic instincts in all living creatures: survival. Normally, survival instinct is stronger than the wish for destruction."

Beneath the doctor's words, hiding behind each of his statements, I sense a kind of conviction, as if he's sentenced me to house arrest for ten years, or as if he were only revealing a thousandth part of the drama that awaits me.

"Remember what I've said because it's fundamental: all failed suicides regret their attempt immediately after. This is because, however tired they may feel on one particular day, the following morning they always find the strength to carry on fighting … at least for a while. So, whenever your wife thinks about death, ask her to wait another day and, when she thinks about it again, ask her to wait a second day and, if it's necessary, a third, a fourth, a fifth, until she stops saying that life causes her pain."

The doctor insists on this idea because he wants to be sure I've understood that, from this moment onward, my existence will transmute into a state of perpetual tension. For the next ten years, every evening, when I come back home, I will walk down the corridor with the fear that my wife may be hanging from a lamp hook, diving in the bath or agonizing inside the closet, and every morning, when I head for the laboratory, I will look at her as if for the last time, remind her that I love her and close the door with a heavy heart like a mourner when he sees how they lower the lid of the coffin or, to be a little more precise, with the same anguish that took hold of me when, at the age of eleven, after my grandmother died, I had the impression we'd buried a woman who was in fact only sleeping. This thought nurtured my habitual obsession for death to such an extreme that, for a week after the funeral, whenever nighttime plunged the house into the utmost silence, I could hear with absolute clarity the noise her nails made scratching the sarcophagus and the muffled scream with which she repeated my name from the cemetery where she would now surely perish. For the next ten years, as I head toward the laboratory, I will experience this anguish and, for the rest of the working day, I will call my wife every five minutes, I will remind her I love her as much as I did that morning and I will invite her to come and have lunch with me at the university, holding back the tears when she replies that today, just as yesterday, the day before yesterday and the day before that, she doesn't feel like leaving the apartment. This is how my future will pan out in the best of cases. In the worst of cases, of course, there won't be any reason to feel anguish.

"How will I know she's thinking about death?" I ask.

"She's your wife. You're supposed to know what she's like."

The doctor has said this with cruelty and immediately afterwards, perhaps because he's sorry for the harshness of his statement, he gets up from his chair, places himself in front of me and sits on the edge of the desk. I do not like his attitude. He is not my friend, my father or my doctor. In fact, I don't even know his name. So I'd prefer him not to be so close.

"From now on, you're the only person who can get the idea of death out of her head. There's no one else at your side. Don't forget: you're alone in this."

He becomes even more serious when he adds:

"It's not easy living with a suicidal person."

And repeats:

"Not easy at all."

And reaffirms:

"Not easy in the slightest."

At exactly this point, there is a loud bang on the other side of the door, followed by an insult and shouts growing louder all the time. There is obviously something going on outside, but the psychiatrist, who is determined to give the impression he's in control of the situation, doesn't flinch. Not until he becomes aware of my uneasiness and informs me that the staff in this center are perfectly used to dealing with patients' hysterical fits. As can be imagined, this explanation doesn't exactly reassure me. Because a man like me, who spends his days analyzing insects and his evenings swallowing TV, cannot deal with so many emotions in such a short space of time. Today I've seen my wife dying inside a closet, I've had a run-in with the witch next door, I've endured the wisecracks of two paramedics, I've recalled my childhood traumas, I've discovered there are nutcases in our midst and we don't even realize it, I've been sentenced to ten years of unremitting tension and, on top of everything else, I am now in an office and the door is being forced by the same loonies who a moment ago were behaving serenely. Now how the hell am I going to be calm? Even if I try to appear composed, in case the doctor starts to analyze my body language, I cannot stop the muscles contracting under my skin and beads of sweat trickling down my forehead. I am just picturing myself grabbing the psychiatrist's lapels in order to plead with him to intervene before this bunch of maniacs knocks down the door when the uproar suddenly ceases. A moment ago, it sounded as if the waiting room were the scene of a pitched battle, but in the twinkling of an eye the racket has faded and the doctor, maintaining the position he adopted before the scandal broke out, continues haranguing me as if nothing had ever happened:

"I've ordered your wife's admission to hospital as a matter of course. We always place suicidal people under observation for twenty-four hours because this is the riskiest period. We have to be sure that the patient has given up the idea of harming herself. Do you understand?"

I do not answer.

"My advice to you now is to go home and think about what I've said," he adds.

"Can I see my wife before I leave?"

"No."

The psychiatrist is categorical about this and, to show that he will not yield to my demands, he returns to his seat behind the desk. He doesn't even change his mind when I repeat my request a second, third and even a fourth time. In fact, as I'm pleading with him to allow me to talk with my wife for even half a minute, he looks toward one of the drawers and, ignoring my pleas, rummages about it searching for some papers I have to sign, he explains. But I'm not going to give up so easily. I need to say good night to my wife because for the last five years I've always kissed her goodnight before getting into bed and I don't think either of us will be able to fall asleep if today, under the present circumstances, we break with our routine. I do not mind imploring a fifth time that, for the love of God, he allows me to talk to Elena, and nor do I yield when the psychiatrist, shielding himself behind the impossibility of contravening hospital rules and regulations, explains that a large number of patients blame their relatives for their misfortunes, and so the center, for the first twenty-four hours at least, prefers patients not to have any kind of contact with the people who make them think of death. I have to admit that his argument is irrefutable, although I am not to blame for my wife's actions. Or at least that's what I think. On the other hand, to tell you the truth, I can't say I'm sure of anything anymore. Perhaps Elena considers me the direct cause of her unhappiness, and I haven't even realized it. Who knows. Right now, everything appears confused. So confused I decide to ask whether my wife has said anything negative about me, and the doctor, who is unmoved by my concern, replies that he is sworn to secrecy. He looks at me strangely, as if challenging me to guess what lies behind those buttons his profession has given him for eyes or savoring the power he derives from his white lab coat, and stares again at the drawer.

"Today is our wedding anniversary," I remark as a last resort.

"I know. I've spoken to your wife. But that doesn't change anything."

He pulls out an authorization form for her admission and, before I can express my disagreement, warns me that, if I refuse to sign, he will request the judge to place Elena Domingo under the guardianship of the hospital.

"You mustn't think we enjoy doing this," he says. "Apart from the reason I explained to you earlier, there are other motives for keeping patients in twenty-four hours after their attempt. To start with, there are suicidal people who decide to abandon this life by turning on the gas in full knowledge that the building will explode as soon as a neighbor presses the doorbell. Lots of people are angry at society, you know, and we have to protect the local community from such bitter characters. But there's another motive: money, my friend, damn money. In this hospital, we have plenty of experience pumping out stomachs of old people who've been encouraged by their heirs to take more than the usual dose of sleeping pills. We have to protect these people as well. You do understand me, don't you, Mr. Garrido? You do understand?"

Again, silence.

"Until we've had a quiet chat with your wife and the police have taken her statement, we won't be able to discharge her. And that's all there is to it."

Having pointed at the papers he's placed on the table, he suggests I sign them right away. But his arguments are not enough for me to give up on Elena, so I stare into his eyes, take a deep breath and, for the last time, ask him to make an exception. At this point, he appears to hesitate. For a few moments, the psychiatrist observes me with interest, as if surprised by my pigheadedness, and I'm finally able to make out a face, a real face, emerging from the cloth ball on top of his shoulders. The insistence with which I have tried to show him I really need to talk to Elena has softened his heart and, paradoxical as it may seem, I am suddenly invaded by a terrible fear of having to face my wife. I think I went on at the doctor because this is what any good husband would be expected to do, but in reality I lack the courage to confront somebody who right now, in spite of five years of marriage to her, strikes me as a complete stranger. The fear of sitting down next to a woman who possibly accuses me of having nourished her sadness reminds me of the panic I felt when the neighbor of my childhood set one foot on the railing and let a few seconds go by before coming out with the comment see you later, Julito. I often think she said goodbye to me because, deep down inside her soul, she wanted me, full of innocence on account of my age and therefore able to restore an adult's hope in a better world, to say something that made her hold back. But I remained quiet. The situation struck me as so strange that I stared at her without opening my mouth. After that, it was too late. Needless to say, over the years that followed, apart from having the idea that people would rather throw themselves under the wheels of a bus than put up with my presence, I also arrived at the conclusion that words could save lives. But instead of talking nineteen to the dozen, as would have been logical under the circumstances, I became a child who always looked inward, and never outward. At the age of eight, I was so impressed by the consequences of my silence that, always unconsciously, I understood my lips would never emit a single comment that would be useful to others and, although the passage of time has partially eroded this belief, I am still convinced that my vocal cords grow stiff in certain situations. This is why I am terrified by the possibility of not having anything to say to my wife, and so I cross my fingers, hoping that, in his capacity as psychiatrist, this man will understand I'm not ready to talk to Elena. I want him to play his role by pretending he realizes that, deep down inside, I do not wish to confront the patient, and in return I will play mine by giving the impression I'm furious he won't let me. Unfortunately, the doctor doesn't seem prepared to play along. Quite the opposite. He seems actually to be considering the possibility of making an exception in my case, and my legs are already trembling when I notice the doctor puts his hand over his mouth once again as if he were zipping up his lips, and then I understand that this man would never allow a relative to visit one of his patients during the first twenty-four hours, but gives the impression he's hesitating because he just loves tormenting people like me who pretend they are tough guys without having really thought about what would happen if they were left alone with people who blame them for all their misfortunes. If this doctor really does enjoy causing such suffering, he must now be in seventh heaven. Because I'm going through hell. And I'm still sweating blood when a gigantic security guard bursts into the office, goes over to the dummy and whispers something in his ear, at which point everything speeds up. The psychiatrist suddenly grows impatient, sticks a ballpoint pen in front of my nose, orders me to sign the document and places his hands on the desk in what is clearly meant to be an intimidating gesture. The specialist is trying to hurry me up because something is going on with the lunatics in the waiting room, but I still have enough energy left to pretend I object to not being allowed to spend five minutes with my wife, so I click my tongue in disagreement and fold my arms without taking the pen. When the porter, however, places a hand on my shoulder and tells me to sign the fucking piece of paper at once, damn it, I obey. Then, as the same orderly is pushing me toward the exit by shoving my scapula, the psychiatrist points out that the following evening, diagnosis permitting, an ambulance will take my wife to our house. A few seconds later, I find myself in a waiting room that is completely empty. The vast number of patients occupying all the chairs have disappeared, but the receptionist is still standing behind the counter as if nothing has happened and only reacts when she sees me staring at her open-mouthed. Only then does she wish me good night, smiling widely and holding a finger in front of her mouth so as to stop me asking any inappropriate questions.

From the street, I have a quick look at the automatic doors of the psychiatric emergency ward. My wife will spend the night in a building that swallows people up, I think, and I am immediately overwhelmed by the desire to retrace my steps and get her out, whatever the cost, of a place where doctors lose their features and patients the guardianship of their families. Renouncing a husband's legal authority feels like betrayal, and I am terrified by the thought that they may stuff her with so many pills they will change or even annul her personality. I've seen too many films in which doctors trepan skulls, fix eyelids or lash wrists, and find it easy to imagine Elena banging on a door covered in locks, calling my name down the corridors of this madhouse or being molested by a bunch of lunatics she's forced to share a room with. These fantasies make me want to rescue her so much I decide to go back into the hospital. I take a step forward, which causes the automatic doors of the lobby to open, and the receptionist, seeing me standing in front of the door, shakes her head, which makes me step back immediately. I have refrained from doing what I wanted because someone who didn't know what I was going to do has told me not to do it, and so I stand in front of the building, feeling more stupid than ever. I am still tormenting myself about my inability to carry out my plans when a loud hoot brings me back to reality. My body is in the way of an ambulance whose driver gestures to me to get out of the way—I can clearly make out the words "you idiot" on his lips—and I immediately step to one side so that the vehicle can come to a halt and a paramedic, different from the one who welcomed Elena to the paradise of second chances can jump on to the tarmac, pull on the stretcher where a man is dozing, let out a shout, gesture something, greet a doctor, make a remark I cannot hear, deliver some papers and hand over to a porter who pushes the stretcher toward the psychiatric emergency ward of the hospital I have just abandoned. A moment later, the paramedic turns to face another person, I imagine the new arrival's wife, who seems to want to thank them for saving her husband's life. But this woman is unable to utter a word, so the paramedic pats her on the shoulder, points to the building and, needless to say, asks her to be a good girl and wait in the waiting room. A few seconds later, the ambulance disappears around the corner and, having watched the whole scene unfold in silence, I stare at the woman, who returns my gaze with a terrified look verging on hysteria similar to mine a couple of hours earlier. But, instead of offering any consolation, I quickly turn around and walk away.

3

I want to believe that, in a few minutes, when I open the door to our house, I will wake up from this nightmare. Elena will appear in the corridor and ask me how my day has been. She will hang up my jacket in the closet, order me to sit down at the table, switch on the television, mutter something on her way to the kitchen, and everything will be as it always was. Or as it nearly always was. Because tonight, when she's least expecting it, perhaps when she's cooking dinner, I will go up behind her and whisper in her ear life would be horrible without you. And, after a moment's confusion, she will feel happy. I suppose she will say something to evade the subject, because she doesn't know how to react to a declaration of this caliber, but deep down inside she will be pleased to know that I'm in still love with her, after all these years still madly in love with her, and she will never again want to die. I want to believe that, in a moment, when I finally cross the threshold of our apartment, life will give us a second chance, one I plan to make the most of, for example by declaring my love for Elena at all hours of the day, by taking her into my arms and reminding her she's not alone, she has me, here I am, darling, always at your side, always with you, always needing you. I want to believe that at this very minute, when I finally enter the house, the hands of the clock will turn back a few hours, canceling my wife's entry into hospital, the ambulance, the closet even, and allowing us to correct the mistakes we've made during our marriage. I want to believe all this will come true. But none of it happens. Because there is no one in the hallway. No one except for the silence and the pair of rubber gloves the ambulance men left where the two corridors intersect. Not wanting to believe anything else, I head toward the bathroom, prepared to take a relaxing shower, and, as I get undressed in front of the mirror, a mirror I have shared a hundred times with my wife, I study the ravages of time on my body. The once robust young is now a man without appeal. Muscles lacking in tone, gray hair behind the ears, budding breast-like pectorals. For many years I have felt flabby, spongy even, in other words extremely unattractive. What's more, for some time now I've felt embarrassed to appear naked before my wife, so, whenever we make love, which isn't very often nowadays, I always turn off the light. Years ago, I used to enjoy watching her half-closed eyes as I thrust myself between her legs, but now I prefer to merge with her shadow in order not to see the disappointment in her eyes after I've penetrated her. And when I finally come on top of the sheets, never between her thighs, Elena gets up from the bed, enters the bathroom and, with legs slightly arched, she wipes her vagina with toilet paper. In the beginning, when we were still proud of our bodies, we played at making out shapes in the little pools of semen I deposited on her belly, but after a while, I cannot say when, our love-making came to its climax with Elena sprawled

74

on top of the toilet bowl, wiping herself with a Kleenex down below and closing the door when she caught me peeping. My wife detests her anatomy as well. Although the passing of the years has not deformed her excessively, perhaps only what you would expect in a woman of her age, she regards her body as a hindrance and so, whenever she enters the bathroom, not only after making love, but also under other circumstances, she locks the door. Before she lost her job, we used to share the bathroom because we didn't want to waste any time out of an absurd sense of modesty and the only time we respected each other's privacy was when one of us was using the toilet. But then, after her depression settled in our marriage, she began to bolt the door, and never again did we give each other little shoves while brushing our teeth. When I realized that my wife had acquired the habit of locking herself inside, I kept silent. I pretended not to notice something that was obvious, and barely a month later, perhaps a little longer, our marriage had become filled with padlocks. It was round that time when we started pretending not to notice things that were evident, such as dinners eaten in total silence or her visits to the widow next door, and it must have been around then that we planted the seed of the accident, the damn accident that took place this evening.

As we speak, tired of contemplating getting flabbier by the minute and of analyzing the mistakes committed during several years of marriage, I prepare to take a shower, but I've barely put one foot inside the tub when somebody rings the doorbell and, with the towel tied around my waist, I wander down the corridor, trying to imagine who could possibly be disturbing me at two o'clock in the morning. A few seconds later, having glimpsed the doorman's silhouette through the peephole, I deduce that the neighbors have sent this henpecked husband to gather information about the day's events and I curse the moment I ever rented this apartment plagued with false Samaritans. Before opening the door, I think of a lie I can use to get by without having to confess the business of the suicide attempt—Elena sprained her ankle while placing a box in a top cupboard or fainted because of the strict diet she herself decided to go on with the aim of losing weight. But, having finally confronted the janitor, who doesn't stop scratching his bald patch, I realize I won't need to invent any lies because he clearly prefers not to interfere in my life. Not in mine nor in anyone else's. I only have to look at him scratching his head to understand it was his wife, a busybody if ever there was one, who sent him up to my apartment to return the chair left in front of the building as an excuse and bring back a comprehensive report on the reasons for an ambulance carrying off my wife. Fortunately, this poor wimp is unfamiliar with the tactics of getting people to talk and, since he appears unwilling to learn, he waits for me to tell him about it of my own accord, which obviously isn't going to happen. To make matters worse, as I wait in silence, a cough betrays the presence of the caretaker's wife on the floor below and, incapable of hiding my feelings at the absurdity of this scene, I adopt a weary expression that the janitor doesn't fail to notice. He looks first to the left, as if pondering something, then to the right, as if seeking to refute his previous argument, and then to the ground, as if finally making up his mind to confront his wife, the gossip that life, together with a certain amount of bad luck, has saddled him with. He then points to the chair sitting on the landing, wishes me good night and, having scratched his crown again, disappears from my sight. While I am happy to find out there are still individuals who don't give a damn about other people's lives, I am immediately sorry not to have told him what happened. Because I sense the consequences of my silence. Tomorrow morning, when the neighbors discover I refused to say a word, they will invent their own version of the facts. First, they will weigh up the truth about the indigestion the paramedics mentioned to the widow on the seventh floor; then, they will come up with an alternative, let's say that Elena suffered an anxiety attack on account of her work situation; and finally, in need of greater emotions than these, they will concoct a far more convoluted story, such as that I beat the daylights out of her, or she suffered a shock on finding out I'd been unfaithful, or fainted when she found pictures of naked children in my briefcase. And once they've drafted the complete version, a text to which they will add such juicy details it will be impossible not to believe, they will direct all their wrath toward me. They will be so horrified by the work of fiction they themselves have created that, refusing to admit their ability to devise such a convoluted plot, they will accuse me of having taken part in events that only ever existed in their imagination and, during the following weeks, while pulling minor variations on the main theme of their fantasy out of their sleeves, they will eye me with genuine hatred. They will express their hostility whenever they take the elevator with me, whenever we meet in the street, in short, whenever the opportunity presents itself, and I will only manage to get them off my back when I tell them what really happened. Only then will they shut up for good. Because the day they find out everything that happened, when they truly learn the facts and there is no reason to speculate, they will not want to hear another word about it. When they realize that Elena wasn't beaten, that I wasn't unfaithful, nor do I keep child pornography in my briefcase, and so that my wife lost the desire to live for no particular reason, they will be afraid something similar could happen to them and their families, and this will terrify them so much they will automatically stop gossiping about us and focus their attention instead on the retard from apartment number two on the fourth floor, or the homosexual from number one on the fifth floor, both essential characters when it comes to the neighbors regaining lost ground.

I know my neighbors will behave like this because that is how the tenants of my childhood behaved toward the widower whose wife jumped over the balcony. I remember, in the months after her death, people spread such nonsense about the reasons for her leapfrogging the railing they went so far as to consider the possibility he had pushed her himself. I was their eyewitness of everything that had gone on, but some even dared to doubt my version of events by arguing that eight-year-olds interpret reality as they please. These individuals never admitted that their despicable behavior was not out of respect for the truth, but because they needed to fill the void of their own existence by toying with the life of others, and for a long time they took on the role of judges, inflicting an exemplary punishment on the supposed culprit of the accident. That is, the widower. As if this were not enough, the great instigator of all this injustice was my own mother. In her desire for revenge for the toll this had taken on her son, my progenitor substituted the events I had narrated with a series of lies that instead of explaining the truth distorted it to such a point that it was utterly impossible not to end up hating Manolo. The fact is her lies had a great deal of success in the neighborhood. My mother was an expert at slander and everybody in our building reached the conclusion no tenant could ever withstand circumstances anything like those endured by the dead woman, which somehow made us all immune against what the woman in the baker's had begun to call "balcony sickness". People loved listening to Mrs. Garrido's version of events, in particular the way she painted Manolo as a dullard or his wife as a suicidal maniac stuffed full with the only pills against depression that existed back then, which were obviously highly ineffective, and our neighbors liked her stories so much, I think, because they insulated them from the possibility of raising a hand against themselves. Since they couldn't understand what motives would drive somebody to jump off the fourth floor, they came up with an awful life for the couple—for which it goes without saying they had absolutely no proof—which allowed them to go to bed convinced that no member of their own families would ever commit such an act as that of the deceased did by jumping on the mailbox, basically because there was no dunce husband in their homes, they felt no infinite sadness in their hearts, they didn't even have a plant pot hanging from the ceiling of their balconies. In fact, the neighbors needed less than two months to tarnish the reputation of the widower, who probably spent the following years suggesting his wife had stumbled because he sensed these rumours at his back. Nobody displayed even a hint of compassion toward this man who was, after all, mourning the loss of his spouse. The most they did was pat him on the shoulder to get rid of him whenever he started with his lamentations, but nobody ever said we're here for you, Manolo, nor did they console him by suggesting no one is to blame for the actions of a suicide. They never did anything like this, nor did they accept a plausible explanation for the reasons that led this woman to leap into the void, but invented a shitty life for the couple and withdrew into their homes to carry on with their own shitty existences. That was until the day I hit the roof. It happened one afternoon when, having wet myself three times in a row to the great amusement of my fellow students, I ran into my mother chatting to the owner of the bakery located beneath our balcony, a woman who also hated the widower not because he'd done her any wrong, but because she needed someone to blame for the splashes of blood that had become ingrained in the shop window on the day of the accident. When I entered the shop, the two women were fabricating a story about the suicide that had nothing to do with reality and, since it seemed to me that distorting the facts was somehow distorting me, I interrupted their conversation by shouting at them that their story was nothing more than a filthy lie—the neighbor never insulted his wife, that afternoon he didn't call her a dirty slut, she didn't threaten to take her own life, he didn't reply go on and jump then, you fat bitch, and the fat bitch didn't then say to me, before

80

launching herself into the void, that in a few years you also will turn into a complete bastard, but instead of this whispered in the voice of an angel see you later, Julito, and jumped over the railing without donning the white wings she undoubtedly deserved. I clarified these points because I didn't want my story—that is to say, the story that would somehow constitute my personality—being distorted by a couple of women who didn't dare look at the naked truth and, after a few moments' silence on the part of my mother, instead of apologizing for altering my circumstances, she slapped me so hard that I still feel my cheek burning. Then, as she went on rapping me on the back of my neck while pushing me up the stairs, she ordered me never to contradict her in front of her friends and added that, if she said a pig could fly, I should always and at all times confirm that pigs can fly. Then, to make sure I'd learned the lesson, she impressed her words on my brain by dealing me such a blow I climbed three steps in one go. That same afternoon, I decided to leave home as soon as I was of legal age and, while feeling sorry for my father, a man who was completely crushed by marriage, I also decided to break off all links with a woman I continued to call "mother" out of obligation rather than affection.

Although the shower washes my reminiscences off my body, the towel brings them back to my head with greater intensity. What water took away comes back with dryness, exactly like the fear of abandonment that vanished after my adolescence resurfaced during my marriage. The parallelism between that time and now is becoming increasingly obvious, such similarities worrying me enough to imagine, just to imagine, that the child I was once appears in a corner of the mirror and, staring at me with fierce eyes, asks me what I have turned him into. Detecting a certain amount of resentment in his words, resentment I will absolutely not tolerate in such a little squirt, I reply rather tactlessly that his relationship with suicide will not be limited to the plunge of the lady next door, but in a few years, when he's least expecting it, when he really isn't expecting it, I could even say when he's not expecting it at all, the whole thing will happen again. Then, when the little boy has grown pale on account of my premonitions, I add that his battle against traumas—a battle that by now he should be waging alongside psychologists ill-equipped to help him—this battle—I go on—will be nothing but a waste of time. I imagine the child who once lived inside me bursting into tears behind the mirror, in the same manner and posture in which I am weeping in the middle of the bathroom, but I cannot stop the flood of sincerity that has taken over me, so I bring my face close to this window on the past, carefully scrutinize my own pupils and, searching perhaps for the child that survives inside me, I mutter that this is what your future is like, Julito, and there's nothing you can do to change it, nothing, unless you do not marry Elena, something I wouldn't recommend, I wouldn't recommend at all, in spite of being aware of the current circumstances, the horrific current circumstances, because she will give you the best years of your life, do you understand? The best years of your life you will receive from a woman who will try to abandon you by entering a closet, but you won't mind because a kiss from her lips, a single kiss from her lips, will more than compensate for the ten years of uncertainty

I—not you yet—will have to confront as of this moment. I reveal all this to the child I believe I am talking to and, a moment later perhaps, almost without realizing I'm the one moving my lips, I hear the child ask, in a voice again laden with resentment, what I am doing to prevent my wife, the woman whose kisses give me so much happiness, from ending like the lady next door who jumped off the balcony. And this is how, aware that I do not have an answer for such a question, I understand that at the age of thirty-five I cannot stand still, as I did aged eight, waiting for adults to show me how to deal with the problem. There is no longer a mother obsessed with revenge, nor classmates pointing at the fly in my pants, not even shrinks more concerned about covering their couch in towels, in case I pee on the upholstery, than about freeing my brain of its traumas. All these useless people have exited from my life, and this allows me to do something I could never have done back then, which is to take action. Instead of standing still, waiting for help from adults who aren't really all that interested in lending me a hand, I can fight tooth and nail to win back a woman who, unlike the neighbor suffering from balcony sickness, didn't die in the attempt. And it is at this precise moment, when the child there was once inside me is beginning to fade, when I swear I will do everything in my power to understand my wife's motives.

Having dressed, I scour the house in search of clues to help me understand Elena's behavior. I have already inspected all the rooms a couple of times when it occurs to me my wife must have left a farewell note somewhere. I rummage behind the furniture in the living room, in the bedroom and my study, but, as I turn out the drawers with the growing conviction there is no holograph to be found, I start to feel dizzy. The idea that my wife could not have spared me a thought before deciding to abandon this life upsets me so much I have to hold on to the bookshelf in order not to lose my balance. And when the stifling sensation turns into breathlessness, the breathlessness into trembling, and the trembling into tightness, I open the door to the balcony to inflate my lungs with a huge gulp of air. I stagger back into the living room and, having sat down, am again overcome by dizziness, as if hundreds of fingers were banging on my chest, which makes me stand up and walk around the room, more out of a need to move than for any other reason. In spite of this, the malaise persists. I do not wish to stay still because I am afraid, really afraid, that all this tension is going to cause a general breakdown in my organism, so I gather all my strength in order to continue searching for a farewell note and, since it occurs to me that Elena might have hidden it inside a book with the idea that I would find it in some remote future, I fling myself at the bookcase, take out a novel, flap it in the air and throw it on the floor. I grab another book, then the following, after that this one back there, proceeding with the one right next to it, then the one on the other side, and the next one, and so on, and so forth, and more of the same, and continue dismantling our library for half an hour, possibly three quarters of an hour, even more perhaps. After a while, having finished with this piece of furniture, but still prey to the sense of unease, I place the volumes back on their respective shelves in such a way that I end up arranging the books, and that takes me the same amount of time as before, perhaps a little less, I do not know, and, having finished, I scour the house, hoping to find another possible hiding place for this stupid farewell note, searching for it again—if in truth I am searching for it—in the bedside table, in the suitcase kept in the top cupboard, in the kitchen cupboards, under the bed, in the laundry basket, in the shoeboxes and lots of other receptacles whose contents I scatter all over the floor without consideration, even experiencing a certain amount of pleasure at the resulting disorder, as if taking revenge for the obsession of my wife's symmetries or the insults I receive every time I spoil one of these perfections. I then move on to the next room, stepping on all the junk that's in my way, sometimes crushing it, and I go on until anguish takes complete hold and I end up not only causing havoc in the apartment, but tearing down the curtains, dashing pictures on the floor, kicking walls, ranting and raving about those fucking shrinks unable to foresee panic attacks in their patients' relatives, smashing glasses on the worktop, breaking broomsticks, banging on the gas pipe, banging on the gas pipe again, banging it a third time in the hope that the building will finally explode, punching the doors with my fists, emerging on to the landing to curse the neighbors, those fucking gossipmongers, going back into the apartment with the intention of destroying more furniture and, in a final outburst of rage, having broken the hangers of the closet into pieces, rummaged through all the clothes and torn my wife's best outfits, returning to the living room, shaking out the books again and, in a raging fit of hysteria, unbinding thirty, forty or even fifty volumes. I am still in a maelstrom of destruction when, having stopped to catch my breath, I feel a tightness in my chest, as if someone were trying to strip off my shirt—in this case a shirt called the soul—and this forces me to kneel down in the middle of the room, vomit up to the tiniest particle of food in my stomach and reach the conclusion I'm on the verge of a heart attack. I think I'm going. I don't know where, but I feel I'm about to leave my body, so I huddle my knees in an attempt to stop anybody ripping out my life, I plead with God for an extension that is sufficiently long to allow me to help my wife get better, and I try not to lose consciousness activating my brain with mechanical thoughts, such as remembering all the Spanish rivers, the chronology of Gothic kings or, something that is easier, the nine times table. And at the point I feel a twinge in my lungs, I say nine, eighteen, twenty-seven, while making a superhuman effort to drag myself to the phone—thirty-six, forty-five, fifty-four— with the intention of calling emergency services—sixty-three, seventy-two, eighty-one—something I am unable to do because I momentarily lose consciousness—ninety, ninety-nine, one hundred and eight—just for a moment— one hundred and seventeen, one hundred and twenty-six, one hundred and thirty-five—and then recover it immediately, look at my watch, only to discover that nine hours have passed, nine long hours, since I suffered that fainting fit—one hundred and forty-four—that so closely resembled a heart attack.

I gingerly get to my feet, not wanting to black out again, and can still feel my bones are stiff when I notice it's three o clock in the afternoon. I should call the university to inform them about the reasons for my absence, in case the dean, who doesn't like me that much, should decide to cancel the grant I received two years ago so I could detect, study and prevent the invasion of the tiger mosquito. I should phone him at once, but at this point in time I don't much feel like talking to anybody, least of all someone like him. Also, given the state the house is in, I should really clean up this mess before Elena, on her return from hospital, discovers that, where she created order, there is only chaos. For the next two hours, I pick up the things tossed all over the floor, I even glue back the pieces of a couple of objects broken during my outburst, and, having finished, I go downstairs for a breath of fresh air. There is still half a day to go before they give me back my wife, long enough for me to take a stroll through the city and relax daydreaming. And so I head off in no particular direction. Everywhere I go, I see men in bars, old people on benches and women on balconies. Sometimes, when I focus on their faces, I notice a strange look in their eyes. Perhaps they are sad, or absent, possibly they don't know where they are going. I sense these emotions because I have acquired a sixth sense for grasping pain, a human being's deep, authentic, insurmountable pain, and I only need to pay attention to their pupils to realize they are gagged by frustration. During this walk on which I constantly observe the features of others, I detect an enormous number of people who are sentenced to life, something like passengers in transit, and I am horrified to recognize in them the same weariness that I've seen on Elena's face for the past few months. I continue like this for about an hour, with every step I take feeling more and more shell-shocked by the reality that meets my eyes, when, after a while, having left the more populated avenues and entered the less busy side streets, I end up in the neighborhood where I grew up, just a few feet from my old house, a stone's throw from the balcony the neighbor of my childhood threw herself off. A homing instinct has brought me to this place because deep inside me I want to find out what happened to that husband whom nobody supported during the time he was mourning his wife's death. I want to learn how long it took him to rebuild his life, how he got over the feelings of guilt, when he recovered the love of life, where he keeps the memory of his wife and, above all, why such a disaster happened to him, and nobody else but him, although it also happened to me a little bit. I need answers to these questions because I sense that this guy's present hides the keys to my future, but at the same time I'm terrified to come across a man who has been destroyed by life. I don't dare face the crystal ball this man must have in place of a head, so I immediately turn around in order to leave this place, but then I discover a square to my left, a square that brings back memories of games shared before the age of eight, needless to say, with other neighborhood kids. After that, once the neighbor had launched herself off the terrace, I gave up playing catch, hide-and-seek and football in front of the church for ever, partly because I was afraid of wetting myself in public, but also because I knew that my friends' parents had told them not to hang out with that strange Garrido kid. From one day to the next, the children I used to spend Sundays with stopped pressing the intercom to shout come down, Julito, the guys from the next block have challenged us to a game of marbles, and that was when I stopped enjoying my childhood. It was around that time that I turned into the saddest boy, and later the saddest man, in the world. My friends abandoned me to my fate because grown-ups had forbidden them—lest they be punished—to hang out with a boy who wasn't to blame for what he'd witnessed and, when they caught me watching them from a corner, they looked at each other without understanding why they couldn't be friends again with the team's leading goal-scorer. The adults' inability to understand that I hadn't gone crazy, I was just a little traumatized, is what deprived me for the rest of my days of the joy of celebrating a goal with my team-mates, of dribbling past a dog in the square or passing the ball to a friend, for example the boy who later, in an act of brotherhood that would never be forgotten, shouted at Manolo to stop banging on about his deceased wife because we all knew she'd committed suicide to lose sight of him and, at the same time, to fuck up poor Julito's life. I'm still upset at having been deprived of such simple pleasures. Because I was a good boy, I was really good. I was also really good at everything I did. Not just at playing football, but also at friendship. And yet everything went awry on the day of the balconies, and never again did I shoot the ball into a net protected by a goalkeeper, the most I ever achieved was shooting the ball between two trees with my shadow as the only presence.

Seeing the square in which I had been almost happy immerses my body in a pain that doesn't affect one organ in particular, but somehow damages them all. A pain that I, like the doctor who attended my wife on the psychiatric emergency ward, would refer to as pain in the soul because I have no other way of defining it, but which is really physical pain. And yet, instead of going home to appease my malaise with drugs, I decide to soothe it by confronting the situation I fear. I'm fully aware that the only way to relieve my suffering is to encounter the widower, observe his face twenty-seven years after the tragedy and conjugate the elements of his present with the possible elements of my future. So I pluck up courage, walk toward the front door of my old home and, when I'm only a few feet away, I feel a shiver run down my spine, as if there were a ghost behind me or, to be more precise, as if a spectral hand had stroked the back of my neck. It is then I glance to one side and catch sight of the mailbox, the damn mailbox on which my neighbor lost her life, just to the right of me. And yet what has made me shiver is not that, but the silhouette of an old man in the distance, on the other sidewalk, to be specific, sitting on a bench, disappearing behind a bus and then reappearing when the bus moves on. It is the widower from my childhood. Manolo gazing at the mailbox beside me. Fixing it with those eyes, eyes filled with darkness, set in the middle of a face distorted by grief, possibly the most grief-stricken face that can be imagined, certainly the worst face this world has ever seen. Only someone as naive as me could have hoped he would find a recovered man instead of a wretch with his eyes wide open, as if he were still studying the broken body of his wife, his mouth tightly closed, as if there were words inside him left unsaid, his brow deeply furrowed, as if he'd spent the last few decades concentrating on only one thing, and his ugliness highly diffuse, as if the putrefaction of his soul had been forced to manifest itself in the form of emaciation, poverty and filth. Pain and its sister, sadness, have disfigured this man's body because there was nothing left to deform in his soul, while solitude, together with its stepson boredom, has transformed him into a kind of statue as yellowish as the newspapers, old newspapers, he holds in his hands. But there is something even more depressing about his attitude. Because this human wreck is not in the least surprised that I, a stranger in principle, should check him out from head to toe. His emotional apathy has reached such a level that he doesn't even flinch when strangers gawp at him like a freak and carry on their way with lowered heads, possibly stunned by the cruelty of life as exemplified by this poor devil. The old man, whom I remember on his knees in that mirror-filled elevator, realizes that people are stunned by his sad figure because he also has to confront his reflection in the mirror every morning, and so he understands why everybody, absolutely everybody, shudders on seeing solitude personified in his features. He cares so little about people's interest in his face, which is logically a morbid kind of interest, that he isn't even bothered when, as is the case now, a young man drags his partner to the bench where he is sitting and says listen, Manolo, I've brought my girlfriend to meet you. The old man has only to look in her eyes for the woman, barely more than a girl, to feel utter repugnance, bury her face in her boyfriend's chest and ask him, plead with him, to take her away from there at once. Then, on finding myself alone again with an individual whose mere presence scares away all those creatures who have yet to discover the ugliness that inhabits the adult world, I decide to leave this place, but, before turning the corner, I take one last look behind me and find the suicide's husband, the man who remains in a huddle on account of the dizziness he feels at the thought of rising from the bench, staring at me in amazement, as if he's suddenly realized who I am, and I only have to return his gaze for him, ever the coward, to twist his face back toward infinity represented by the mailbox. I imagine myself retracing my steps, grabbing hold of his throat and ordering him to regain control of his life. Because I do not want any men, men whose wives jumped off balconies or swallowed bottles of barbiturates, to remain blocked for the rest of their existences. I do not want any of this. I insist, I simply do not want it. And yet I don't do anything to change it. I simply set off for my apartment in the shape of a cross, for I am as much of a coward as he is.

I walk down the streets, not seeing anybody around me this time, as if all the men in bars, old men on benches and women on balconies had fled, leaving behind them a city in which I feel terribly alone. From time to time, I hear someone's voice, perhaps a passer-by talking on the phone, or a horn honking, in this case a car braking as I cross without paying attention to the lights. But then immediately silence returns. Together with Manolo's face, that face that prevents me from dwelling on more pleasurable memories, such as my wedding day, the night Elena first told me she loved me or the afternoon I learned I'd been awarded a grant to study the tiger mosquito. None of these memories is strong enough to annul the presence of this man inside my brain, an image that only fades when, at the end of my walk, I catch sight of the building where I live. Just as I think I'm safe from the anguish provoked by a city behind the windows of which

I glimpse hundreds of faces identical to the widower's, many of them pleading with me to free them from the prisons their lives have turned into, just as I think I'm safe from all this paranoia, I spot an ambulance parked in front of the building. Twenty-four hours have yet to pass since my wife was admitted to hospital, but the doctor has discharged her early, probably because he has confirmed that she doesn't plan to harm herself, and he is sending her back to me much as one would deliver a package to a stranger. When I approach the drivers to ask whether they have brought Elena Domingo, they seem unwilling to answer, instead they shoot each other a quick glance, throw their cigarettes on the ground and stamp on them in an extremely cocky manner, after which one of them declares that he finds it outrageous I wasn't at home waiting for my wife to come back. I am just about to reply that the doctor assured me he would release her later when his colleague adds that, at a time like this, the patient needs to feel loved, not spurned, by the only person who is going to be at her side from now on. It is quite clear that these individuals have taken a dislike to me and, since I am fed up of justifying all my actions to complete strangers, I limit myself to showing them the door of the building and telling them to get a fucking move on and take Elena upstairs. A few seconds later, still with an expression of distaste, but understanding that the best way to be rid of me is doing what I tell them, the two men head toward the back of the ambulance, open the door and, having said something to my wife I cannot hear, they help her out of the vehicle, at which point I go up to give her a welcome kiss which she, as was partly to be expected, receives with

93

chilling indifference. The four of us then enter an elevator that is too narrow for so many people and, on the upward journey, the paramedics and I avoid touching each other or exchanging looks by squeezing into separate corners. We are all huddled together when, on passing the fourth floor, we notice a face pressed against the window, that of the mother of the retarded boy from apartment number two, who must be thrilled there is a new rumor circulating about another tenant, since this will temporarily tune down the gossip concerning her son's habit of masturbating in the early morning in front of apartment number one on the third floor, home of an eleven-year-old girl the silly boy is head over heels in love with, to put it mildly.

But in this building gossipmongers do not run the risk of extinction. No sooner have we reached the seventh floor than the widow from the apartment opposite appears on the landing—as usual, as if by magic—and, throwing herself at my wife, she covers her in kisses two, four, six, eight or even ten times. The old woman clinches the patient with such devotion it's almost obscene and the paramedics, pleased by such a show of affection, do not let the opportunity go by without casting me a disapproving look. The coldness with which I greeted my wife contrasts sharply to the warmth shown by the neighbor, and this situation makes me so angry I feel like slapping this old woman who is able to shed such a clear light on my emotional tepidity. Fortunately, it won't be necessary to push this old fogy aside, since she herself draws back on seeing the apathy of Elena, who blows neither hot nor cold in spite of the enthusiastic greetings, but displays an indifference identical to the one she showed me when

I kissed her by the ambulance. My wife is sufficiently sedated not to have a clue what is going on. She's been given so much medication she can't even control her jaw, and the sight of her gaping mouth makes me think that the hospital, that admitted an intelligent woman, is sending me back a lobotomized female. There is no doubt that my wife will return to normal as soon as the effects of the substances temporarily administered by the doctor to placate her unfortunate delusions have passed, but the old woman, who doesn't realize the strength of sedatives that have been so generously injected, despairs on seeing how her friend ignores her endearments and, concluding that her adored neighbor will never be the same again, she covers her face with her hands, takes a few steps backward and, letting out a groan that would send a shiver down the spine of the dead in the cemetery, she finds shelter in her apartment. The truth is that, for the first time since I met her, I feel sorry for the old hag. I've never been that bothered about the Methuselah's loneliness, nor was I concerned about her dependence not only on my wife, but on anyone who was willing to spend a bit of time in her company, but at this point in time, hearing her crying behind the door of her apartment, I share her pain and decide to extend a bridge between us by inviting her to come to our house for tea the following afternoon. So, while the paramedics are taking Elena into our home, I reach out to ring the old lady's doorbell and have just pressed it when the widow opens the door, gathers some saliva in her mouth and taking aim, lands a gobbet of spit, no doubt the most accurate gobbet ever ejected, directly on my forehead. She then takes refuge behind the portico of her fortress and, from the entrance hall, she calls me "monster from hell", "bastard offspring of a three-tailed devil" and, most strangely of all, "son of a thousand-headed whore". Needless to say, as the witch proceeds to spit out insults that are little more than esoteric, my blood boils. I would like to strangle her with my belt, kick her head in or disfigure her with my teeth, but I can't waste time with medieval gargoyles like her, so I wipe the spit off with my sleeve and enter my apartment, where one of the paramedics stares at the mess, while the other, who is probably more used to the pigsties inhabited by regulars of the psychiatric emergency ward, explains to my wife how to take the drugs the doctor prescribed for her. He asks if she's understood and, since Elena's mind is still so cloudy, so cloudy she doesn't even object to the chaos in the living room, the paramedic snorts, gets up slowly and heads toward the front door without saying a word. When they are both on the landing, I go out behind them and wait for some kind of comment, even just a brief summary of the doctor's diagnosis. But they don't say anything. They hand me a piece of paper on which someone has scribbled the doctor's phone number, but they do not utter a word, nor do they recommend a course of action, they don't even say goodbye. These guys couldn't give a damn about my presence because they don't consider me part of their job, so they merely stand there waiting for the elevator while giving the impression they haven't even realized there's someone there. And yet I need an explanation, a diagnosis or an instruction manual, I don't care, something that will show me how to behave as of this moment. And since I'm really in need of some kind of explanation, I try to encourage the paramedics by holding out a twenty euro note as tip, just in case they're avoiding me because they think I'm stingy, but, instead of taking the money or rejecting it politely, they stare at me with obvious contempt. They then enter the elevator. But, before they disappear for good, I block the door with my feet in order to ask:

"What do I do now?"

The shorter one, who is also the more cruel of the two, replies bluntly:

"Look after her."

Which his colleague, who absolutely concords with this shitty diagnosis, backs up by saying:

"That's right, look after her."

The door closes, and, with my face a couple of inches from the window, I stare at their bodies being swallowed up by the shaft. A few seconds later, when I'm alone on the landing, a cough re-echoes down the stairwell. Probably the janitor's wife. Although it could also be the woman from the fourth floor, anxious to spread a rumor that will divert the community's attention away from her first-born, the aforementioned retard-cum-pervert.

4

All of a sudden three days have gone by since my wife sought the confines of the closet. In all this time, we have avoided talking about what happened, letting the television chat in our place and even turning a deaf ear when, on a tabloid talk show, a guest described his grotesque attempt to hang himself using his mother's pantyhose. But yesterday afternoon, tired of being reduced to silence and sick of wallowing in my self imposed listlessness, I phoned the doctor on the psychiatric emergency ward to ask him for advice about the best way to bring up the subject, and no sooner had I let out that I still hadn't dared discuss the matter of suicide than he exploded, angrily accusing me of being irresponsible and urging me to make an effort to show Elena she had married a man, a real man, and not a coward incapable of dealing with a new situation. Having thanked the physician for the sincerity of his words, an acknowledgment to which he replied by abruptly hanging up, I planted myself in front of Elena, determined to regain control of our marriage, but, before I could express my wish to have a conversation about the events in which she starred on the night of our fifth wedding anniversary, my wife abandoned the sofa, claiming she needed a shower, and ran to hide in the bathroom, from where she didn't emerge for an hour and a half, during which time I wandered up and down the corridor, first preparing a speech about the importance of restoring communication between us, then going over the dialogue I had had with the psychiatrist on the night of the closets, and finally counting the boards in the parquet floor—fifteen, they were, if I remember correctly. After considering that enough time had elapsed since Elena entered a bathroom where, in addition to bottles of shampoo, there were also nail scissors, razors and other sharp objects, I pressed my ear to the door to make sure my wife was still moving and, having confirmed she was still alive, I headed to the fridge, determined to prepare some dinner. Dark thoughts, however, had found their way into my mind and, when I opened the kitchen drawers, I was overwhelmed by the large number of knives and toxic products that could be transformed into lethal weapons in the hands of somebody suffering from the so-called "balcony sickness". The chance that Elena might harm herself using one of these utensils affected me so much I threw all the knives in the garbage can and was just emptying a bottle of bleach when I glimpsed my wife's silhouette in the doorway, a silhouette, needless to say, with a face displaying a look of contempt that was so sincere, so utterly sincere, I considered for a moment pouring the alkaline solution all over her face. I'm not sure how long we remained in this position, her staring at me with eyes swollen with disdain and me pouring the contents of the bottle down the drain, but, after the final drop had disappeared down the plughole, Elena stretched out her arm, pointed at me with the remote control handset and pressed the "off" button. Not the button for the volume, for changing channel or for using the mute, but the "off" button and no other. Then, no doubt disappointed by the fact I hadn't vanished, she returned to the sofa from where, with the same handset, she switched on the TV. Obviously, I didn't want to waste this opportunity to place myself in front of her and ask, almost on the verge of tears, how I could help her get out of the pit she had fallen into, but I only got silence for an answer. Even so, I insisted. I tried again because I needed answers to all the uncertainties aroused by her attempt at self-injury, so I insisted once again, this time in a fit of tears, and would have done so a third time if, at that precise moment, she hadn't picked up the handset, pointed toward my belly and changed channels through my body, revealing in this way that, while she couldn't turn me off, she was perfectly qualified to ignore me.

Our misunderstandings did not end with the incident yesterday afternoon. Because a few hours ago, noticing the lack of provisions, I tried to persuade my wife to accompany me to do some shopping, but, making use of her increasing verbal frugality, she simply said no. Then, as I remained paralyzed, not knowing how to tackle this new crisis, she recommended I get used to leaving her alone because, you know, darling, you can't keep an eye on me forever. I realized she was right. Her observation forced me to accept the impossibility of controlling her actions always and at all times, since I had no choice but to adapt to current circumstances, in particular to accept the fact that the continued existence of my wife would depend only, absolutely and exclusively on her, and on nobody else. Our society's demands would force me to leave her side at any moment: the dean would require my presence in the laboratory, the neighbors would organize another gathering in the staircase, her brother would invite her to lunch at his house or, something much more silly, but at the same time more realistic, like the rolls of toilet paper would run out and somebody would have to go out and buy some. In short, life would demand my incorporation into normality at any moment, forcing me to trust my wife to stay by herself without committing some stupid act or, failing that, in the strength of anti-depressants to stop her having suicidal thoughts. And since Elena's words have made me understand something so simple, today for the first time I have undergone the suffering I will have to endure every time over the next ten years when for whatever reason I am forced to leave her side. Judging by the result, I predict a decade of anxiety. Because my quick getaway was a disaster. I had intended to return home in less than fifteen minutes, but needed more than three quarters of an hour to fill the shopping basket, wait in the supermarket queue and rush along the streets back to my apartment. To begin with, I enjoyed perusing the aisles of the supermarket, since the shopping frenzy of the establishment took my mind off reality, as if the satisfactions of consumerism, with its offers of the week and discount coupons, had suppressed the concerns that in the past tended to occupy citizens' heads, concerns such as making ends meet, problems with alcohol overindulgence or anxiety triggered by wives displaying a readiness to slash their wrists as soon as they are left by themselves. For several minutes, I forgot my fears, but after a while—to be specific, while waiting my turn in the queue—the image of my wife once more showing the whites of her eyes on account of barbiturates resurfaced in my brain more vivid than ever, and I was no longer able to calm down. To make matters worse, the girl at the cash register, a useless specimen, performed her work with staggering ineptitude. The girl ran the optical reader over the barcodes without any of them registering on the computer and, even though it was obvious the scanner wasn't going to work, the young girl, never thinking to use her pretty little fingers to key in the numerical sequences stubbornly insisted on using the damn machine. She tried to smooth the packages by hand to make the labels legible, but the more she tried, the more the queue's impatience grew, a queue that got longer and longer, and the nervousness and hence the clumsiness of the checkout girl increased, creating a vicious circle it was impossible to break. At a certain point, no doubt fed up of waiting, a customer spat out to the girl get a move on, for fuck's sake, we haven't got all day, words that were echoed by other customers, who didn't refrain from calling the woman idiot, retard and fucking moron, putting her under such great stress that the products started falling out of her hands. I was just about to add some insults of my own when the supermarket manager, a boy around the same age as the girl, replaced her at the cash register with the arrogance of someone who believes they alone can right an injustice. Only then did the queue begin to move and, barely ten minutes later, when the cashier had checked through five customers in front of me, I asked him please to hurry up because my wife was very ill and I had to get home quickly. This was a mistake. Because the squirt, perhaps taking me for the leader of the previous mutiny, decided to avenge himself on all troublemakers through my person. First he started blowing bubbles with his chewing gum, then he pretended the computer was broken and finally, of course, he attempted to run the optical scanner over all the products, again without using his pretty little fingers to key in the numbers. When I asked him a second time, for Heaven's sake, to hurry up, the guy eyeballed me with aversion and asked the previous cashier, the inept bungling idiot, to return to her post, which delayed my exit from the shop for another five minutes.

Having abandoned the supermarket, I took off in the direction of my apartment and would have arrived in a flash had I not, on turning the penultimate corner, bumped into my neighbor's dog tied to a lamp-post, the same mutt that spends every spring barking and every summer getting kicked, the same animal that always forces me to bow my head whenever we stare at each other from our respective balconies, the same mongrel that dozens of times has humiliated me before the presence, not to say indifference, of my wife. On bumping into this flea-ridden mutt in the middle of the street, I imagined its owner was in a nearby shop and, needing somehow to express the rage that had been pent up inside me over the last three days, I stamped my heel on one of its paws causing an immediate howl at which several pedestrians, alarmed, turned around. But on this occasion it didn't bother me being the focus of everybody's attention. Not even when an old man, lifting his cane with the same malice shown by my wife when she picked up the remote control, spat out that only cowards abuse irrational beings, or when a baker brutally similar to the one from my childhood abandoned her establishment to announce her intention of calling the police. None of this bothered me. In fact, quite the opposite. The sight of the mutt's bleeding paw, its nails uprooted, its pads hanging from their tendons and its long hair matted on account of the blood, as well as the prolonged vision of the pain impressed upon its features and the hatred clearly visible on the faces of passers-by—a hatred in every way stronger than my hatred toward the dog, but equivalent to my mother's hatred of Manolo— the sight of all these things, it seems to me now, gave me pleasure, a pleasure that bordered on ecstasy as I reveled on finding out that I could take action against those who barked at me, threatened me or simply complicated my life. And I felt an even greater satisfaction on confronting the baker who had threatened to call the police, since I didn't spare the old man a glance, by suggesting she refrain from sticking her nose and her croissants in other people's business, you filthy gossip, because I've had it up to here with people like you, people who blabber on about others in order to fill their own lives, their repugnant, disgusting, boring, shitty little lives, I'm sick of all that rabble, you stinking fat-ass, so stop pushing me around and shut your fucking trap unless you want a baguette up your ass. And although this woman stared at me as if I was raving mad, I felt overjoyed at finally giving voice to words that had been stuck in my brain since time immemorial. I felt even happier when I glanced at the dog, the old man and the baker, then at the dog's paw, the old man's stick and the baker's hairnet, and finally at the dog's broken claws, the old man's broken wrinkles and the baker's broken lips—in

105

her case from so much gossiping—and only then did I fully understand the latent aggressiveness that existed inside me, an aggressiveness that must have been increased by the current circumstances—the horrible, frightful, stressful current circumstances—and it was then I understood what the psychiatrist meant when he told me that Elena needed to feel that she could count on a man, Mr. Garrido, a real man. Because a moment ago, when all this happened, and in particular when I realized all of this had truly happened, I considered myself, perhaps for the first time in my life, a cool guy. My behavior pleased me so much I would have stayed beside the mutt, waiting for its owner to appear— whom I would have loved to kick in the mouth in the same way I had stamped on his pet's paw—but the fear of wasting precious time pushed me homewards, bursting with joy at my new personality, head held high, as if I'd suddenly turned into an extraordinary man, or as if the years of looking inward, and never outward, were finally coming to an end. In such a state of euphoria, I crossed the threshold of my apartment and headed for the living room, where I found Elena sitting on the sofa, sitting on the sofa again, with the television in the background, and I didn't even put the shopping bags down before snatching the remote control handset from her hands and saying:

"Get ready, because, like it or not, we're going to talk about your suicide attempt."

My wife is dumbfounded on hearing this demand, which I made a few seconds ago. She probably can't work out where I found the strength of character to raise my voice and, just as she opens her lips to say something, perhaps to say something really important, such as the motive that led her to try to take her own life, the reason she planned to abandon me in the worst possible way, a way as horrible as entering the closet with an overdose of barbiturates in her stomach, my cellphone rings, and the name of my laboratory assistant flashes on the screen. My heart skips a beat. My assistant only ever calls when she has news of capital importance, so I look at Elena in an attempt to convey my uneasiness, maybe asking for a five minute truce, and put my ear to the receiver in order to hear a voice, Nuria's voice, shouting we found it, Julio, we found it! It is obvious I require no further explanation to understand she means the tiger mosquito, the longed-for dipteran known scientifically as *Aedes albopictus*, an insect I have followed in body and soul, though perhaps more in soul than body, during the last two years of my life. My associate gives vent to her joy—we got it, Julio, I swear to you this time we got it!—while I remain as rigid as a statue, my eyes fixed on the ceiling, my fist clenched around the phone, thanking the heavens for finally rewarding the suffering endured not only during the last three days, but also during a life of traumas and solitudes. I gaze at the lamp in the corridor as if that light symbolized the pupil of God's eye or—why not?—as if the light bulb itself concealed the smile of my neighbor, by which I mean the acrobat from my youth, who has returned for the occasion from the depths of hell, which needless to say is a Dantesque hell where the souls of suicides spend all eternity squirming in trees planted in the so-called "wood of suicides", in order to give me the good tidings announced by my assistant. At this point, I clearly recall when I was eight years old, having witnessed this woman's descent and spent four days weeping in my room—which my mother forced me out of by the way, wanting me to return to normality as soon as possible—at the age of eight, as I was saying, I became convinced that the dead woman's ghost, however paradoxical this may seem, had turned into my guardian angel. I don't know how I ended up transforming the person responsible for all my ills into the bearer of subsequent gifts, but the fact is, four days after witnessing her fall, my brain made reality more palatable by picturing the lady's soul repenting of the evil consequences her act would have on my pre-adolescent mind, and that same night I dreamed that the dead woman, or rather the dead woman's spirit, sneaked into my bedroom, sat at the foot of my bed and promised me to make up for such a dirty trick in the not too distant future. As was to be expected, the passing of the years watered down this image in the chiaroscuros of my memory, or so I thought until now, when recollections of my guardian angel flood back into my head and I find myself being blinded by the light bulb in the corridor while thanking her for intervening in the possible capture of the first tiger mosquito in this country. I am still directing my thoughts toward the other world when I half hear Nuria's voice trying to tell me that the director of a clinic contacted the university yesterday afternoon in order to inform them of an increasing number of consultations on account of mosquito bites not normally found in that region. The doctor contacted us because the rashes experienced by his patients were too swollen to be caused by a local mosquito, apart from the fact that the victims had been attacked during the day and on various parts of their bodies, something that would be unusual for indigenous dipterans. In any case, when I finally come back to reality and look away from the lamp, I urge my colleague not to start celebrating too soon, since there are plenty of insects capable of producing similar symptoms to those of the tiger mosquito, at which point Nuria, probably offended by my lack of trust, replies that she has e-mailed me some pictures of the rashes identified in the clinic. We carry on talking while I open my e-mail account, download the images and confirm immediately that my assistant has not jumped the gun, the swellings on the patients' arms are identical to those skin reactions after an attack of *Aedes albopictus* shown in entomology manuals and we are a step away at last from professional glory. That's when I start shouting we got it, Nuria, we got the damn bastard!

A wide variety of insects travel from one country to another thanks to the constant flow of merchandise from one part of the planet to another, but there is no doubt it is the tiger mosquito that has profited most from such commerce. During the last two decades, this Asian dipteran has colonized so many nations it has turned into a real nightmare for numerous governments, which invest all sorts of resources in order to bring the plague under control and curse themselves for not having prevention programs in place that would have enabled them to act as soon as the first specimen was found rather than when the colony was nearly at its peak. Fortunately, certain countries have learned from the mistakes of others and are paying whatever it takes to locate a specimen as proof that colonization has started, after which they can activate a system for containing the plague that is much cheaper and more effective than any extermination program begun at a later date. When I presented my thesis on the subject of this well-known dipteran, which I became enchanted with during a class on invasive species, it didn't occur to me that the Ministry of Health, together with that of the Environment, would be prepared to subsidize a monitoring program for this species, but my wife urged me to broaden the scope of my work by recommending to the relevant authorities the creation of a department in charge of controlling the expansion of an insect capable of procreating in millions of places and of transmitting malaria, at least in warmer climates. A few weeks later, the faculty dean welcomed me into his office to ask whether I would be prepared to manage the budget that had just been assigned by the Council of Universities to the search for evidence of the presence of this insect in our territory. It goes without saying that I answered yes. Then, after we'd shaken hands, the dean winked at me while adopting a confidential tone and assured me that adding the bit about malaria on the last page of my thesis had been a brilliant move. And I thought you were stupid, he remarked. But the dean wasn't as clever as he thought he was. The real reason my proposal was approved was not fear of such a disease spreading, but fear of having to spend more money if no action was taken in time. I am absolutely convinced that the sum granted for my project was given because of a note attached to my report, which explained that the municipality of Rome spent twenty-five million euros a year fighting a plague that not only upset the local population and increased health spending, but also kept tourists away, as well as a letter written by an Italian biologist claiming that the government could have spent six times less if it had created a laboratory with the express purpose of detecting the first colony of tiger mosquitoes in the country, and a second report by an internationally renowned economist raising the possibility—owing to the increasing number of Asian products being imported into the European market—of certain invasive species—one of them being the tiger mosquito—becoming a real burden on community members and having a considerable impact on the budgets of countries unprepared for such an invasion. Undoubtedly, the reference to malaria must have frightened the civil servants, but there's no way it could have had a similar effect on the scientific experts who advised the bureaucrats on the suitability of devoting such funds to my project, since any entomologist worth his salt knows that, for a disease to be transmitted, the disease first of all has to exist. And there is no malaria in this country. Even so, the Ministries of Health and the Environment heeded my warning about the need to create an information network with me as focal of any rashes different from those caused by indigenous species, at which point a preventive system could be put in place, designed for the occasion. Three months later, having almost forgotten about my proposal and started looking for work in private companies, I was awarded the funds I needed to start my research, given a box-room in the faculty basement and assigned an intern, Nuria, to help me with my work.

The first part of a research project on an invasive species such as the tiger mosquito consists in calling every single hospital, chemist and clinic in the country and asking the person responsible to inform the researcher as soon as they come across an unusual rash on the skin of their patients. For the first four months, I devoted myself full-time to making numerous phone calls, endeavoring always to talk to the person in charge, to whom I would give a spiel about my work until I was sure they appreciated its importance. None of those on the other end of the line objected to working with us but I did notice a certain indifference to my words, as if they were bored or didn't really comprehend their significance, and I couldn't work out the reason for such a couldn't-care-less attitude until I visited a local office of the Ministry of Agriculture, where I found a notice-board plastered with requests similar to mine: the search for a settlement of Geranium Bronze; a plan for the mass poisoning of Argentine ants; the rules of conduct when confronted by red palm weevils; a map of the colonies of oriental fruit moths; and so on, and so forth. There were myriad investigations concerning other equally invasive species, to which could be added the petitions of a group of biologists—a bunch of lunatics according to the rest of the scientific community—who were determined to prove the existence of transgenic insects let loose on the world by unscrupulous multinational corporations. The realization that my project was just another drop in the vast swamp of grants awarded by the government, combined with the certainty that four months of calls had fallen on deaf ears and I was devoting myself to the discovery of a minute insect in a huge territory, took the wind out of my sails, but once again it was my wife who revealed the capacity she used to have for encouraging me and told me I should feel proud to form part of a group of scientists whose research was of national importance. Five minutes after listening to her words, I regained my enthusiasm, shut myself in the "creepy-crawly room" and wrote down the main points of the second part of my project, which would entail traveling to ports in search of cargo ships carrying stowaway colonies of *Aedes albopictus*. Studies carried out in various universities have shown that the tiger mosquito moves from continent to continent hidden in ship containers, particularly suspicious being ships transporting bamboo canes and second-hand tires, objects which hold just the right amount of water for the laying of eggs. The larvae pass undetected through phytosanitary controls at Customs and, when these vessels reach port, the insects disembark, making it impossible to prevent colonization and only allowing as of this moment a limited amount of control. To tell the truth, the tiger mosquito doesn't destabilize the ecosystem it invades, one could even argue that it makes it more diverse, but its bites are so bothersome that the local population rushes to the clinics in droves, sky-rocketing municipal budgets for public health and driving mayors crazy as a result. This is to say nothing of the media, which immediately reports on the ability of the dipteran to transmit malaria and dengue fever. Of course, as soon as the press, TV news programs and radios start broadcasting the arrival of an insect carrying such illnesses, governments start forking out considerable sums of money. And that's where entomologists like myself come in. I'm convinced that, when the discovery of the first colony of tiger mosquitoes in this country becomes public, hordes of journalists will come running to my laboratory, but I'm also sure that, before I'm allowed to give a single interview, the dean will summon me to his office and remind me of my obligation to give the impression that everything, absolutely everything, every single detail, including what we do not know, is under control. Otherwise, not only will the hypochondriacs of this country suffer a panic attack, but, much more importantly, our grant will be taken away.

Nothing, however, is under control. Every scientific method depends to a greater or lesser degree on chaos, in the company of chance, as is shown by the fact that, less than a year ago, during the second phase of my project, I myself inspected the port where the tiger mosquito has now turned up. I was there, but it didn't help. I went there because the customs officers informed me of the arrival of a cargo ship full of Chinese tires and, before the vessel appeared on the horizon, I was already smoking a cigarette on the quay. I remember when I warned the foreman I would have to check the merchandise before it could be unloaded, waving the documents that accredited my powers over the containers, the man examined me from head to toe, spat into the sea and, wiping his brow with his forearm, gave me six hours' time to perform my task, after which he would order his workers to take the tires to the retreading factory that had bought them. In the beginning, this seemed long enough to carry out the necessary inspection, but when I discovered that the innards of this ship held the largest shipment of tires my eyes had ever seen, I realized I would need more than three days to complete my work, albeit only superficially. My colleague and I spent the whole morning checking five of the thirty containers in the hold and, as the clock struck three in the afternoon, the foreman came in, pointed his flashlight at me and told me to get the hell out. I refused and again wielded the papers that authorized me to retain any vessel suspected of transporting invasive species as long as I considered necessary, assuring him that getting in the way of my work would lead to an administrative sanction, if not a penal one, of no small dimensions. Needless to say, I issued this threat while trying to conceal the trembling in my legs, a trembling that came from my lack of experience in such situations, nor do I need to point out that I carried on sifting through the papers until the foreman spat again, this time against a container, and in all sincerity suggested that it would be a good idea for my own safety not to piss him off. It took me a while to react. The situation was far too embarrassing for someone like me, who is unused to confrontations, and I was just getting ready to yield to my opponent when it occurred to me, almost by chance, to mention the word "malaria", at which point the sailor's features contorted. Such a seasoned traveler understood perfectly well the implications of this disease, having no doubt, in the past, witnessed the moans of a fellow seaman or even suffered them himself, and he took a few steps backward, looked around as if searching for ghosts and, having slapped the back of his neck, probably because he thought there was a bug buzzing around there, he came back to where I was standing. He rolled up his sleeves, revealing two arms like hammers, and, just as I thought he was going to smash my face in, he asked me to inspect them in search of bites. A moment later, after I'd assured him more than five times that there were no suspicious markings on his skin, he abandoned the hold, informing me that the owner of the import company had called to ask about the reason for the delay in unloading the merchandise, which suggested he would soon turn up on the quay himself to oversee operations. This guy doesn't give a damn about mosquitoes, he added. After this, my assistant and I spent the next three hours working flat out, but in that time only managed to inspect another four containers, after which a man dressed in a jacket and tie burst into the hold, came over to where we were standing and identified himself as the manager of the retreading factory. I only had to look in his face to realize he wasn't going to be intimidated so easily. The old-timer clearly understood that, if we discovered a breeding ground of *Aedes albopictus* in his hold, we would place an embargo on the containers for weeks, and he wasn't prepared to let his business go to ruin for such a reason. He ignored our explanations and ordered us to leave the ship at once, backing up his words with a glance at the two mechanics-cum-gorillas at his back. When I showed him my accreditation from the Ministry of Health, my opponent, with a show of calm disguised as politeness, lit a cigarette, read the letterhead and, tracing a smile on his face that could have come from the devil himself, assured me that he now knew where I lived. He then pointed to the exit. And I obeyed. Of course, I obeyed. In fact, I obeyed without thinking twice about it. Barely a year later, when I still feel inside me the anger I felt back then, an anger directed toward my cowardice rather than the individual in question, one might even say a contained rage similar to the one that has accompanied me all my life, the tiger mosquito has been found in the vicinity of this same port, and it infuriates me to think that I, only I and nobody else but I, have facilitated the colonization of our national territory because of my pathetic lack of character.

A few seconds after remembering the event, I order my assistant to book a couple of rooms in a hotel in the affected area, to pack the instruments we will need and to cancel any appointments for at least a week. I then hang up, take my address book and am about to start ringing the official bodies involved in my project when I look at myself in the mirror and realize that right now, as my efforts of the last two years are bearing fruit and the time approaches for me to show my worth as a field scientist, I am a man on a mission. I know what I have to do and I do it without hesitation. I behave naturally, without getting too carried away, calm and composed like a true professional. I'm the man of the hour. There is no doubt about it. And nothing is going to stop me. No rubber traders, or wives' depressions, or dogs tied to lamp-posts. I'm not going to let such stupidities—which is what I consider them—block my way and will take whatever decisions are necessary in the coming weeks— the normal time required for the capture of a dipteran—to remove any obstacles from my path. I seize the phone and dial the number of the head of the biology section of the Superior Council of Scientific Research. Having heard a greeting on the other end of the line, I break the news that I, Julio Garrido, have discovered the first colony of tiger mosquitoes in our country. I say this statement in a loud voice because this is the official announcement of my discovery and also because—why deny it?—I feel utterly proud of myself. But I am totally stunned by the reply I get:

"The what of what?"

Only then do I understand that I haven't discovered penicillin, or nuclear energy, or even a vaccine against cancer, but a mosquito, a tiny mosquito, one could even say a ridiculous mosquito. I'm not going to allow myself to be overwhelmed by a sense of insecurity, so I reflect on the answer I've heard for a couple of seconds before realizing that, while I thought the phone would ring in the director's office, I am in fact talking to the janitor of the building, and I immediately demand he connect me with the person in charge.

"Who should I say is calling?"

"Julio Garrido."

"Julio … what?"

"Garrido."

"What did you say you'd found?"

"The first colony of tiger mosquitoes."

"The … first … colony … of …" the man repeats, and I realize he's jotting it down, " … mosquitoes."

"Tiger mosquitoes. Don't forget the tiger bit, it's very important."

"Tiger? What have you found? Tigers or mosquitoes?"

"An insect called a tiger mosquito. They're not two separate animals, just one. A tiger mosquito. Do you understand?"

"Yes, man, I get it. Don't get mad. I've got it all written down. Not to worry. Right now I'll go and see if the section head is available. Just a moment, okay?"

"All right."

"I'll be back in a moment, all right?"

"I'll wait for you."

"Don't hang up. Please don't hang up."

"I won't, sir, don't worry. I won't."

When this stranger places the receiver on the table, I strain my ears in order to find out what he's doing. I can't hear any footsteps, or words, or even movements, and I come to the conclusion that the janitor hasn't taken me seriously and isn't going to put me through to anyone. I can make out a slight hum on the other end of the line and picture him with his feet on the table, his hands behind his head and a broad smile on his face. I stay for five minutes, literally five minutes, with the receiver pressed against my ear before I finally hear his voice:

"It would seem the section head can't talk to you right now. He's in a very important meeting. You know what kind of meeting that is, now, don't you? You get it, right? You get what I'm saying, right?"

I can't work out what the hell is the matter with this man, but I mustn't tell him to go to hell because I need him to connect me with his boss:

"Of course, I do," I reply. "Always trapped in a meeting."

"It's unbelievable."

"It is."

There is then a moment's silence.

"Listen, when do you think his meeting will end?" I ask him eventually.

"Oooh, you never can tell. Sometimes these meetings last for hours, others they end in ten minutes. It all depends on the climate."

"The climate?"

"That's right, the climate. The climate is the main thing in these meetings."

I tell myself not to insult this man. I mustn't insult him.

"Well then, I'll call back in half an hour."

"As you wish. Here we are, at your and God's service," he replies. "Oh, and watch out for that mosquito. Don't let it bite you. That would be funny, now, wouldn't it? You'd become the first person to be infected by a tiger mosquito bite in this country. Then you really would be famous! Imagine how famous you'd be. Much more than the guy who discovered a cologne or something … You know, in that case, the section head might even interrupt his meeting."

He seems about to hang up when he adds:

"And don't forget to buy some mosquito repellent. It works very well. Very well indeed."

Fortunately, when I dial the next number in my address book, I reach somebody who only has to hear the dipteran's name to assure me that the following day he will put things in place for me to receive all the help I need. He then hangs up. He doesn't congratulate me, or offer his encouragement, or recommend me for a promotion. His manner is professional and slightly polite. In the same way, during the seven phone calls I make after that, I only detect satisfaction in the faculty dean, whose happiness stems not from the consequences this discovery will have for my career, but from the prestige it will afford his department. But I don't care. Because right now, having phoned all these people and spread the news far and wide, the only recognition I want is Elena's. No other congratulations interest me as much as hers, so I go into the living room, put my arms on my waist and shout I'm a hell of an entomologist, my tracking system has worked to perfection and soon, when news gets around the scientific community about the localization of the first colony of tiger mosquitoes, our lives will take a 180-degree turn. Especially on the financial side, I add.

And yet no sooner have I yelled out all these scenarios than I observe to my horror my wife making an effort to smile. I thought this wonderful piece of news would please her, if only a little, but her reaction is far from fulfilling my expectations. The trouble is, at this stage of her life, my wife doesn't give a damn about anything. Anything, that is, except for the darkness of the closet. For years, I have yearned for professional recognition for the sole purpose of making her proud of me, that was all I wanted, but I am now overwhelmed by a sense of failure that increases when I realize I won't be able to undertake the third phase of my project, which entails moving to the place where the bites have been detected, if she carries on being obsessed with death. My assistant has informed me of the most significant discovery of my career, possibly even the most groundbreaking finding in the recent entomological history of this country, but the circumstances of my marriage prevent me not only from enjoying this fact, but also from seeing the project through. However, after two years of pursuing this opportunity, I don't plan to give it up. I will not let the current situation get in the way of my research, so I try to come up with a solution to my wife's problem, my wife's ill-timed, annoying, irritating problem when it occurs to me that the only viable option involves taking her with me wherever I go. I have no choice but to sign her up to the expedition because, otherwise, she might use my absence to rip off her soul and turn my professional success into an emotional failure, transforming me from the saddest man in the world that has always lived inside me into the most desolate success on the planet. I have to convince Elena to undertake this journey with me, and so I look into her eyes with the intention of informing her, whether she likes it or not, that she must follow me wherever I go, and am just about to adorn this arrangement as a speech on the importance for her health of distancing herself from the city when she, who has always been more perceptive than I am, mutters she has no intention of leaving the house under any circumstances. She then turns up the volume on the TV. Needless to say, I am dumbfounded. I realize I have to deal with this crisis as quickly as possible, mainly because every second implies another set of eggs being laid by the mosquito, and, while I'd like to do this logically, I'm unable to remain sufficiently calm to think clearly. So, instead of sitting down beside her to explain that the success of this mission will bring about a change in our lives, I find myself calling her selfish, a spoiled brat, a silly child, a coward, a slut. Yes, even a slut. I've been waiting for this moment for so long I'm unable to contain my outburst and, feeling the hatred inside me surge to unprecedented levels, I rush to the front door, go out on to the landing, run down the stairs two by two, reach the street, move away from the building, stop at a corner, scream three times, hit a lamp-post and insult every single passer-by staring at me in fear, including the same policeman who, four days earlier, while I was searching for the remains of my wife on the sidewalk, observed me from his patrol car. And having released this resentment built up inside me, just as I'm imagining the policeman arresting me for public disturbance, I feel an imperious need to turn around, retrace my steps and run to my wife's side. And I'm only a few feet away from the entrance when I catch sight of Elena leaning out from the balcony, her head over the railing, the breeze rustling her hair. Although from the movement of her head she is clearly searching for something, probably her husband, I shout to her to get inside for fuck's sake! A moment later, as she withdraws into the shadows of our apartment, I glimpse the widow on the adjoining balcony sticking her nose out of the dark and, in the building opposite, the dog owner doing the same from behind the curtains, holding the bandaged mutt in his arms, staring at me and pointing in my direction in a clear attempt to make it obvious he recognizes me as the dog's assailant, at which all I can do is give him the finger.

After a while, wishing to compensate for my mistake, I invite Elena to have a talk. She looks terrified. She wasn't expecting a reaction like this and she bows her head like a little girl seeking forgiveness for some damage she's caused. My wife was used to the submissive husband she had carefully fashioned over five years of marriage, and suddenly her creature has turned into a raging lunatic who is fed up with obeying her. I haven't taken a single decision in my own home for five years. And I've had enough. Besides, things being what they are, I have to display firmness, not tenderness, so I use this opportunity to ask her straight out whether she still wants to die. I have no doubt, over the last three days, she's thought about it often enough, she may even have felt attracted by the closet on more than one occasion or heard the call of the balcony while pacing the cruciform corridor, but right now, probably because she feels her back to the wall, she says no, I swear I don't want to commit suicide any more, darling, really the idea has left my head. Of course, I don't believe her. I don't believe her, nor should I. Her accident still haunts my memory, and I'm afraid that, if I leave home, albeit for only half a week, she won't be able to resist temptation. When she reassures me that I can leave her alone for a couple of days, she's not going to do anything stupid, in particular when she tries to tug at my heartstrings by using the word "darling" a second time, I reaffirm my position. Had she not called me "darling" twice, I might have wavered, but this term sounds so strange in her mouth, so shrill between her lips, so fake coming from her, that I realize I mustn't abandon her. And I'm just considering a solution to this dilemma when suddenly somebody lights a match in the darkness of my brain. A match that reveals to me the way out of this conflict: I need a babysitter who will stay by her side twenty-four hours a day, somebody who will keep an eye on her constantly, an assistant who understands there is no difference between controlling a child and a suicide, since they are both capable of hurting themselves at the least expected moment. The only person I can entrust this responsibility to, whether I like it or not, is Elena's brother. For the past few months, he's been working in a record shop, a small establishment almost without customers belonging to a friend of Elena's who agreed to hire Juan in spite of his terrible references, because back then, and still now, my brother-in-law was a rake. When my wife introduced me to him for the first time, I found it funny he had a tic which consisted in constantly scratching his nose, but after a couple of weeks, when we were forced to commit him to a detox clinic on account of a cocaine addiction, and when the doctor informed us he was destroying his brain, I stopped being amused and began to feel sorry for him instead. And yet I have no choice but to call him. Although it's obvious this guy, who is currently thirty-two, cannot even look after himself, he's the only person I can trust and the only person who would agree to accept such a task, given that the patient is his sister. When I mention the possibility to Elena, she flies off the handle. She doesn't want her family finding out what happened. The mere possibility irritates her so much she lets out a howl, disappears down the corridor and shuts herself in the bathroom, which has become her own private refuge. I do not flinch at her attitude. I have decided her brother is going to spend the next three or four days with her, so I confront the bathroom door, shout there's no point arguing and move away firmly decided to call him up. A few seconds later, she throws herself at me and begs me not to play such a dirty trick on her, not to worry her family, please not to do this. But even now I'm not going to budge. Quite the opposite. I get her off me, push her against the wall and, with my clenched fist a few inches away from her nose, warn her she's in no position to make demands. She looks at me dumbstruck. She cannot recognize the man in front of her and, no doubt feeling the effects of the blow to her back, she accepts I'm not going to yield to the emotional blackmail implicit in her suicide attempt. But my wife, however, is an expert at adapting to any situation and she launches a counter-attack threatening to divorce me if I make that phone call, a threat that in the current circumstances strikes me as absurd, so utterly absurd I can only interrupt her by saying:

125

"I prefer a divorce to a funeral."

Realizing that my words, however harsh they may seem, conceal a declaration of love, perhaps the most sincere declaration of love I've ever made to her, she collapses on the sofa and bursts into tears.

5

I imagine grief inhabiting every corner of my house. I am on the landing after four days' absence and envisage sadness as a viscous mass festering through the lintel of our apartment, sliding down the door-jamb and oiling the greasy cogs of this lock. Before long I will be part of the pain once more, it occurs to me at this moment, and immediately I perceive the worrying, disturbing eyes of the widow spying on me through her peephole. The woman from apartment two is watching me. I know this because I can sense her smell, the disgusting smell of an old woman, slipping through the cracks in her door, wearing away the colors of her doormat, filling my nostrils and making me retch. A smell of urine, camphor, possibly even liniment. A stink of corpse, threshold of death. If I didn't know the widow was still alive, I'd think this stench, or rather this nausea, originated from her decaying body. But there's no doubt it comes from her gut, passes through her dental pulp and floats across the landing to impregnate my clothes. I imagine this wretch with her eye glued to the peephole, a cat purring at her feet and the rocking chair she recently abandoned on detecting the clank of the elevator swaying in the solitude of her living room, as if a ghost were sitting in it or, much more likely, the devil himself taking a break. And yet the stench is so strong, so perceptible on this landing, that it's easy to suspect the woman was prowling around here recently. At some point in the day, probably not long ago, the widow has visited my wife to sate her desire to know what happened on the night of the ambulance and to wheedle out the truth about her suicide attempt, a description she will no doubt have listened to very carefully in order to garner all the gory details about her agony in the closet, her rescue at the hands of the paramedics and her admission to the psychiatric emergency ward. My neighbor will have thoroughly enjoyed hearing that even I didn't know about this last part, by which I mean what happened during the twenty-four hours Elena remained under medical observation and I was forbidden to accompany her. She must have been overjoyed at owning something I lacked and, in celebration of the fact, she will have launched into an attack on my person. I have no doubt she'll have given my wife her opinion, her repulsive and entirely dispensable opinion, concerning my behavior over the last year, and I'm absolutely sure she will have gone on over and over again about how difficult it must be to find happiness next to a selfish bastard such as myself. I know this old hag will have made such comments because she lets no opportunity pass to insult me—me and any other representative of the male species. I remember when I first noticed her hatred toward men—a hatred revealed by her inability to greet any member of the male gender in the building and by the groans she emitted when the pregnant woman from apartment number two on the eighth floor announced she was expecting a boy, and not a girl—having observed such signs, I remember I attributed her contempt to the anger she felt toward her husband for dying and leaving her all alone. But the passage of time, together with Elena's comments, has persuaded me the witch despised the opposite sex long before her husband's passing, possibly ever since her childhood, or ever since the Pleistocene. In fact, I have never ceased to feel sorry for the martyrdom her husband must have suffered during the years of their marriage, a sympathy that increases every time I calculate the number of cats to have lived in that witch's apartment. Shortly before her husband's demise, my neighbor started substituting the affection of humans with that of felines and, as I've been told, during the wake, which was held in her house so as not to pay a room at the funeral parlor, several times the guests were forced to shoo away a kitten that insisted on parading, as if nothing had happened, all over the dead man's face, causing the make-up to wear away and the true features of death to be revealed. From that moment onward, my neighbor's life has never been deprived of a representative of the feline species and, as the janitor's wife remarked to me not long ago, in the last twenty years, ever since her first day of mourning, the rotation of pets has occurred at an alarming rate, especially when one considers that none of them has lived for more than three years and two of these caterwaulers, by which I mean the white one with black spots and the gray one with an amputated tail, gave up the ghost falling off the balcony, in theory having slipped as they were walking along the railing, proving by their descent that felines do not have nine lives, at least not the ones that get squashed after flying from the seventh floor. I've always found it strange how these cats lost their balance so easily, but even more suspicious is the way the old woman didn't even lift a finger to recover their bodies, so it was the garbagemen who, with a scraper in one hand and a bag of sawdust in the other, removed the corpses of animals whose existence was then reduced to a portrait in the widow's house. On the walls of her apartment, apart from a stench of death and stink of liniment, there are about thirty feline portraits. Over the last two decades, these animals' photographs have adorned the partitions separating the bedroom, kitchen, hall, pantry and other rooms, toilet included, without the same having happened to the images of her parents, children or friends, or even her husband. In this house, there isn't a single snapshot of the man with whom the old hag shared her life, or any of the other people who must have inhabited her past, but hanging from the walls are numerous frames containing the pussycats that have entertained her widowhood, as well as an empty frame where it is to be supposed the photo of the kitty currently keeping her company will go, whose gravestone will not be found in a cemetery since it's already present in the Dead Pets Society Museum in apartment number two on the seventh floor of my building.

Right now, as the old woman's effluvia blend in with my own emissions, producing a third odor I wouldn't know how to classify, but which is extremely unpleasant— most of all because it forces me to consider the possibility there may be something in the widow's essence perfectly suited to my own—I ready myself to face Elena again. I have only just stuck the key in the lock when I am assailed by the hope that, during my four-day absence, my wife may have become reconciled to life. Perhaps her brother, to whom I entrusted her care against all logic and who came immediately to her aid—a brother who offered to act as babysitter for as long as required and, after I asked him about his addictions, swore he wouldn't drink or sniff or inject anything during his stay in my apartment, but failed to clarify whether he'd got over his problems with alcohol, cocaine and pills—perhaps this brother, who remarked he would use these days of seclusion to go over certain documents he'd been collecting for some time— papers whose content, it goes without saying, I was forbidden to inspect—this brother, it occurs to me now, may have got Elena to reconsider her suicide attempt, helping her reach the conclusion there is no more rewarding effort or praiseworthy undertaking than the struggle to continue living in this world, a struggle that is often fiercer than that of those city dwellers who throw themselves off balconies without caring whether they are being watched by eight-year-olds on adjoining terraces. During the four days I spent working in the town of the mosquitoes, I called my wife on numerous occasions, at least five times a day, and, while she didn't always want to come to the phone, when she did, she sounded reasonably cheerful. The sentences she came out with, which were really just formalities, inspired me with confidence, although I have to admit I may have interpreted her words in a more positive way than usual because I need to feel morally justified to go off again early tomorrow morning. I won't stay home for long. I have to go back to the town to capture *Aedes albopictus*, since at this stage of our

131

investigation, when we've placed traps all over the municipality and the insect is one breath away from falling into our nets, I cannot allow myself a prolonged absence, not wanting my assistant—a girl who is so enthusiastic about the project she probably works on it past midnight— to capture the first specimen before my return and garner the applause that strictly belongs to me. If I don't fulfill my obligations, I will lose the opportunity to acquire a certain renown in the entomology scene, an objective that, if attained, will turn into an academic promotion, one that implies the longed-for chair, that chair in the Faculty of Biology finally, with the corresponding increase in salary, my colleagues' admiration and a little flurry in the press. So my thoughts at this moment, as I push the key to the back of the lock and simultaneously sense the widow's peephole transforming into a large pupil—a sensation that has overcome me recently not only when I emerge on to this landing, but also whenever I go by any other landing in the building, as if my neighbors' doors had turned into living creatures, obviously creatures similar to the Cyclops—at this moment, as I was saying, when I start turning the key to the right, I abruptly realize that my real obligation, my moral obligation at least, shouldn't be with my work, but with my wife. In the present circumstances, I should really be behaving like a tried and true man, with all the virtues that implies, and not like a workaholic. And yet, at this point in time, I also reflect on the fact that this world is not an ideal place, no, it isn't, and so I cannot reject the idea that the correct way to behave, one that will enable us to overcome adversity, if only financial, is not to allow myself to be blackmailed by the current situation, but to perform my professional duties, which is the only way to show Elena that life has to go on, the engine will not stop because of her absence and we are all, every single one of us, dispensable. With such thoughts, I'm not suggesting her suicide wouldn't disrupt things, in particular things concerning me, but failing to meet my obligations would have an excessively adverse effect on our world, our limited, insignificant world behind the door of apartment number one on the seventh floor, since I would get fired as soon as the dean noticed I'd been spending too much time looking after a wife who doesn't have a physical illness, but a mental one, an illness my boss may not even consider authentic, as occurs with so many citizens who continue to regard depression as something that affects people who are either lazy or weak. If I were to place Elena's needs before my own professional duties, the person responsible for my project would fire me on the grounds I have thrown out the window two years' research by allowing the tiger mosquito to escape right under my very nose, immediately colonizing national territory and making the control of the species that much more difficult. And if the dean, annoyed by my lack of professionalism, kicked me out on the street, the situation at home would get incomparably worse, since there would then be two people unemployed, not just one. I have no idea how the relatives of other patients with a tendency to inflict self-injury manage, but I wouldn't be surprised if, driven on by a society that only values work and despises, isolates and marginalizes anyone who is not productive, they found themselves in the same situation of having to abandon their loved ones on the third or fourth day after their admission to the psychiatric emergency ward and live, from that moment onward, with fear in every cell of their bodies. In the deepest, most hidden, most secluded part of their bodies they must store the fear of returning home and finding a corpse where there was once a father, a mother or a child. However that may be, the conviction I must carry on fulfilling my responsibilities doesn't stop me feeling remorse at having distanced myself from Elena for four days, but the truth is I find it impossible to imagine another course of action. Abandoning my suicidal wife is the only way to earn prestige and money, which will surely contribute to our happiness, allowing us to hire the best psychiatrists, buy the most expensive medicines, move to apartments not in the shape of a cross and, in short, achieve every single thing that can be had with a large wad of notes. Which is to say everything. And so, having reflected on all these matters on the landing of my home, with the old woman's gaze permanently fixed on my shoulders, I choose to confirm my decision to meet my work commitments without wavering because I have a wife in the worst state imaginable and, my determination holding firm, I mentally cross my fingers in the hope Elena will understand, in the not too distant future perhaps, that I didn't stay by her side during her illness because I wanted to build a better world for us both. This, and no other reason, explains my behavior. So when I enter the house I am perfectly sure I won't be modifying my strategy regarding her illness and I squarely face a corridor at the end of which I see that the door to the living room is closed, a chink of light showing through a crack. When I enter the lounge, I see my wife lying on the sofa, a cup of tea on the table and the television in the background, and then Juan smoking a cigarette on the balcony, watching the neighbor's dog, I think, and oblivious to my presence. I greet Elena with a kiss she accepts with indifference and go out on to the balcony, where I notice my brother-in-law tapping his feet continuously as if he were agitated, so agitated that, when I touch his shoulder, he veers around and, as the dog in the building opposite starts barking away interrupting his silence of just a moment ago, I see a face distorted either by excessive consumption of drugs or by a lack of them. The fact is no sooner has he turned around than he insists he has to leave at once—I think because he wants to sniff something—and will be back first thing in the morning, before I leave for the town of the mosquitoes, to continue with the care and guardianship of his sister. He enters the living room to say goodbye to Elena, assuring her he will be back in a few hours and embracing her as I wish someone would embrace me. I then walk him to the elevator, where he gives me a meaningful glance before whispering:

"It's a shame she's doomed to suffer."

His remark strikes me as so mysterious I demand an explanation and, when Juan replies I'm not ready to hear the truth, I grab him by the lapels, shove him against the wall and make it clear I don't have time for his little secrets. He mutters there are things I will never comprehend, matters that surpass my capacity for understanding, questions that are too transcendental for the minds of ordinary mortals, after which I can only make as if to punch him in the face, taking advantage of the way he automatically covers his face to stick my hand in his back

135

pocket, steal his wallet and assure him he won't get it back unless he agrees to wait for me in the bar on the corner, where I will meet him in less than five minutes. In such circumstances, seemingly desperate because of the loss of his wallet, where I suppose he keeps a dose of cocaine, he accepts my conditions. I return to the apartment to inform my wife I will be out for half an hour and I am just about to ask her not to do anything stupid during this period of time when I notice the door to the balcony, the one which leads to an abyss of seven floors, is still open. While I'm aware that I should close it, I leave it as it is. I suddenly feel the need to tempt fate. To show Elena that, deep down inside, although there are times I would prefer to deceive myself by forcing myself to think the opposite, I know her continuation in this world will depend on her, only her and nobody else but her. However many obstacles I place in her way, my wife will remain in the land of the living only if she so wishes. I can try to stop it, I can stuff her full of anti-depressants, pay the best doctors, but if she decides to take herself out of the equation, there's nothing to prevent this. Not a closed window, nor the disappearance of knives, nor even the emptying of bottles of bleach. If someone wants to die, if someone really wants to abandon a world they consider rotten to the core, if someone needs to do this before anything else and so prefers to be swallowed up by death than to continue at my side, they will always and at every moment find a way to annihilate themselves. Nothing can prevent those who decide impetuously to put an end to their days. Absolutely nothing. At the most, we can hamper their will, but human ingenuity, in particular the ingenuity of those taking decisions with an iron-clad will, is bound to overcome any counter-measure. So this evening, having observed the automaton still in front of the television, the soulless body my wife has become, I leave the house without locking the door to the balcony. For this reason, I go out of the living room without saying a word and, for this reason, shortly afterwards, while holding back the tears in the elevator, I glimpse the face of the child I once was reflected in the mirror, doing exactly what I am trying to avoid, that is shed tears in the corners of the cubicle. On the journey down to the ground floor, which can only be described as a descent into the heart of darkness, I cannot help watching this eight-year-old boy, the one I believe is frightened by the possibility of past events repeating themselves, events that made him into a child always looking inward, and never outward, and the more I examine this memory, the more I fear the possibility, as I leave the building, of my wife falling down right beside me, splashing me with her blood, staring at me with one eye out of its socket and her brains oozing from her nose as if it were a generous dish of spaghetti. Fortunately, when I get to the street I don't come across a corpse, nor do I catch sight of my wife leaning over the balcony, so I consider myself free to head toward the bar where I've arranged to meet my brother-in-law. I find him sitting in a corner of the bar, biting his nails like a man possessed, apparently on the verge of a hysterical attack. There are six other people in this dive, almost all of whom look as if they spend their evenings in this den precisely because they're so utterly bored of doing so at home, although it's obvious they're not having much fun here either, since I only have to greet my brother-in-law for every single one of them to fine-tune all five senses toward our conversation, greedy for some entertainment to help the hours of solitude and alcohol go by. Tell me what's happening, I order him as soon as I sit down. But, before opening his mouth, Juan begs me to hand him back his wallet and, having recovered it, he heads for the toilet, from where he comes back a few minutes later, his face relaxed, an itching in his nose and his throat in constant movement. It is only then, having satisfied his appetite and sated his addiction, that he provides an explanation. First, he says that nothing will prevent Elena's suicide and, since I am dumbfounded by such a statement, he rounds off this remark by repeating that his sister is doomed to suffer. He says this straight out, as if it were the most natural thing in the world, and then takes a swig of beer, stands up and returns to the toilet, where I picture him in front of the bowl, the paper open and a dose rising up the rolled bank note, a supposition that is confirmed when, sitting down opposite me again, he moves his Adam's apple as if he'd swallowed some marbles. In this state, he continues his speech, with greater confidence, and affirms that death has always been inside his sister, as it has always been inside him. He proceeds to stretch out his arms, move the bracelets out of the way and show me the scars on his wrists, cuts that must have been deep, but didn't put an end to his life possibly because fear caused him to call an ambulance before the twenty minutes that are needed to empty a body of its sanguineous fluid were up. Then, having covered up the stitches on his arms, he produces a folder from his backpack, which I suppose is the one whose contents I was forbidden to see a few days ago, and

138

shows me a sheet full of tiny, microscopic annotations while telling me that, during the four days he spent babysitting at home, he questioned Elena regarding her self-destructive impulse, and her answers confirmed a theory he has been working on in recent years concerning the existence of certain determinant factors in the appearance of suicidal thoughts. He immediately gives me an article to read, a page ripped off from a second-rate magazine about how research carried out at some university apparently proved the existence of a genetic, and hence hereditary, component in autolytic behavior. Juan talks to me about triple-blind experiments without stopping to think he is speaking with a man whose scientific education enables him to see past such headlines and place news items like those in the appropriate speculative context. It is obvious he hasn't realized it because he keeps on pulling out cuttings, more and more cuttings, without paying attention to anything except his own paranoia. The lunatic in front of me places papers on the table while moving his Adam's apple up and down and from time to time—when he gets a rush from the nose candy, I think—he points to phrases marked with a highlighter, such as "biological determinism", "serotonin levels" and "localization of neurotransmitters", hoping to impress me and without noticing that I do not see a genius before me, but the typical blockhead who believes he's in possession of the truth simply because he's connected four articles printed in different magazines. And yet my brother-in-law thinks he's revealing a great universal truth, so he carries on with his theory about my wife trying to take her own life simply and solely because she possesses the same genetics as he does, genetics that can only be described as rotten, Julio, rotten on account of a gene, a nasty little gene that drives those who have it toward death, toward self-destruction, toward annihilation of themselves. Then, insisting on sharing with me what he considers to be a proven fact, he pushes the cuttings to one side, covers his mouth to stop the other customers hearing and whispers that, in the history of humanity, there have been numerous suicides who passed on their death wish from one generation to the next, adding immediately that the tendency to injure oneself jumps from parents to children very easily and does so because of something in the genetic code that fails to disappear, but continues with the children of suicides and acts independently of environmental factors, it being demonstrated, Julio, demonstrated that, while suicidal tendencies may be encouraged by negative experiences in life or by an education which emphasizes the idea that taking flight is the best response to situations of conflict, they are transmitted from parents to children, from grandparents to grandchildren even, in the same way as a propensity to cancer, a heart attack or any other hereditary disease, and that is why we cannot blame suicides for an attitude that doesn't really depend on them, but is determined by chance or, if you prefer, by genetic determinism, determinism that causes the onset of this cancer of the mind which some call suicide, an extremely virulent cancer, a cancer you can't fight against, do you understand what I'm saying, Julio? People with suicidal tendencies are not mentally ill, they're physically ill, because their genetic code is damaged, not their brain, and the sad thing is there's nothing you can do about it, nothing you can do about Elena's chemistry, nothing you can do about my chemistry, nothing you can do about the chemistry of our hypothetical children, do you understand? There's nothing you can do about the chemistry of our children because it's inevitable we would transmit the gene whose job it is to make them jump off the balcony at some point in their lives, and that is why neither Elena nor I have ever thought about having children, hadn't you realized, Julio? Were you not surprised that, after five years' marriage, Elena never brought up the subject of having children? Had you really never thought about that before? No, I see you hadn't because you're always absorbed in your work, always obsessed with your work commitments and not your conjugal duties, Julio, that's something you've been guilty of ever since I've known you, so you don't pay attention to things that are obvious for other mortals, but you fail to notice, until now at least, because, thanks to my words, you are paying attention, you are beginning to see that people like us, by which I mean Elena and me, don't want to have children because we know we will abandon them on the day we slash our wrists and also because we're aware—listen to me carefully, please!—we're aware that, as of a certain moment, our descendants will start to hate life for no particular reason, they will hate it simply and solely because they were programmed to reject this life from the moment of birth, it's in their blood, in every drop of their blood, in every cell, in every particle, do you understand? Do you understand? Who would want to have children if he suspected they would try to kill themselves as soon as the gene responsible for ordering self-destruction becomes activated? Tell me, tell me, if you know a single person who would want to have children in such circumstances, Julio, tell me one … At this point, my brother-in-law takes another swig, frowns and carries on taking cuttings out of his folder, old cuttings from six, seven, even eight years ago, which gives me an idea of when this man must have made his first suicide attempt and when the first signs of madness I am now seeing appeared for the first time. Juan piles more and more bundles of papers on the table while exclaiming—shouting almost—that suicides are not to blame for wanting to end their lives, it's not our fault, Julio, you have to understand voluntary death is like any other epidemic, like an influenza that, instead of making your temperature rise, increases your desire to abandon this world, like some fucking virus that has been transmitted from one generation to the next for such a long time, has spent so many millennia passing from one body to another, there's no longer anything you can do to prevent it, no stopping the wheel, no way of holding it back, because hundreds of thousands of suicides have procreated down the centuries, causing this gene, known as the gene of tryptophan hydroxylase or the gene that controls the enzyme that regulates serotonin levels, and also other genes such as the one responsible for … hang on a minute … ah, yes … here it is … receptors 5-HT1B and 5-HT2A, as well as 5-HT1A and probably a few others … as I was saying, suicides have carried on procreating until causing these genes to spread through all humanity, and by now there is nothing you can do about it, do you understand? There's absolutely no way of stopping the expansion of suicidal tendencies on a planetary level, unless you ask those who are affected not to procreate, not to perpetuate themselves, not to have children, Julio, no children, above all no children, because these people's children will engender new beings with the same genes and take their own lives at the most unexpected moment, at least they will want to with all their might, as no doubt happened to one of our ancestors and is happening to us, by us I mean my sister and me, because I'm quite sure my sister and I had an ancestor, probably a great-grandfather, who longed to jump off a precipice, throw himself into a river or gulp down a vial of cyanide, I'm quite sure of this, as I'm also quite sure the thought might have crossed our own parents' mind on more than one occasion, although they've never openly admitted it, I sense my father or my mother, possibly even my father and my mother, may have thought about death at some point in their lives, they may still be thinking about it, but they don't tell us because they think we shouldn't know, they may not even have confessed it to each other, suicidal thoughts make people feel ashamed, Julio, they sure do, among other reasons because they're afraid society is going to label them sinners, cowards, losers, simply because they've had a death wish lodged inside their brain, a thought hammering away at their temples all day long—tack, tack, tack—causing them to suffer in a way that, to make matters worse, they cannot share with anybody, as our parents, our grandparents and our great-grandparents probably never shared it, relatives who never committed suicide, but would, I guess, have liked to, had they not had responsibilities that forced them to remain in the land of the living, because I have no doubt, Julio, I have no doubt that responsibilities, in particular family responsibilities, are what make potential suicides stifle the sounds of those repeated hammerings—tack, tack, tack—their whole life, just imagine what that must be like, our whole life thinking we shouldn't be in this world, we'd be happier in limbo, where we'd enjoy ourselves more if we lacked the capacity for enjoyment, but putting up with life simply and solely because you have family responsibilities and because suicide is considered improper behavior, it is frowned upon Julio, terribly so. Having reached this point, I am fascinated by this madman's ravings. I have before my eyes a total lunatic in all his splendor and, while I suppose I should tell him to get help, I prefer to carry on listening to what he has to say about death wishes, ideas lots of people have from time to time, but we can't get them out of our heads, you have to differentiate between those who have them occasionally and those who have them all day long, because those in the second category are subject to the determinism I referred to and, if ideas of self-destruction didn't stem from a genetic component, Julio, if these constant, permanent ideas of self-destruction didn't come from there, my sister and I wouldn't have tried to take our own lives, it's far too much of a coincidence that both of us have tried, and yet we have, in my case perhaps as a result of the cocaine or the alcohol or the shitty life I lead, I can't say, but something activated that fucking gene at a time when I was happy, I feel like bursting into tears when I think about how happy I was back then, but at a certain point my mind became twisted and I tried to commit suicide on numerous occasions, three if my memory doesn't fail me, once by hanging myself from the hook of a lamp, another by slashing my wrists and a third time by sniffing eight grams in less than half an hour, since one can also commit suicide by taking drugs, you bet you can, it may even be the most pleasant way of doing it, although I can't be sure, since all I managed that day was to get blasted right out of my head and, instead of dying, I ended up in a disco, bouncing up and down, whatever the case I don't try to get rid of those ideas any more because everything has changed since I found out my sister has the same impulse as me, since I found out I am not the only one, I've reached the conclusion it's not my head that's in bad shape, there's something inside me, a gene Elena has as well, which makes me think about death, death, over and over again, hour after hour, day after day, week after week, since that gene makes my neurons focus their activity on ill-fated ideas, and that's why I don't think I'm crazy, I accept the body I've been given, a body with a genetic fault, a body that, if things carry on like this, will cease to belong to me and belong to the worms instead. And so, my brother-in-law continues, it should be clear to you by now that your wife's death, or my own, would only be the result of a natural urge, a gene that in my case was activated long ago, shortly before I was admitted to the detox clinic for the first time, and in my sister's case just recently, when she fell into that depression you've both been fighting against for the last year, a depression that may have no other explanation than genetics, but makes her feel a need to die, a need which is just like any other, like eating, sleeping or fucking, a need that forces her to believe that the human race would be better off if she took herself out of the picture and, if this is what she believes, it's because she's aware, as I am, she has a chemical imbalance that, once transmitted from parents to children, would worsen

145

the human race if she decided to perpetuate herself, have you got it now? I'm talking about an imbalance that leads to premature death, neurotransmitters that don't work properly, brains with rusty mechanisms, mistakes in DNA programming recurring in different generations until they extend to every civilization and which will go on and on and on all over the earth for ever and ever, Julio, world without end, do you understand? It's important you realize that all cultures, absolutely all of them, from Eskimos to pygmies, Chinese to Argentines, Russians to South Africans, all of them have a very similar suicide rate, almost the same in every society, although there is a greater prevalence in advanced civilizations, which leads us to think that suicide is not caused by environmental factors, but by biological ones, absolutely and utterly biological, since otherwise there wouldn't be a similar rate in two different cultures, but the fact is there is and, this being the case, we're forced to reach the conclusion there is a defective gene popping up from time to time, as happens with disorders such as schizophrenia, which has an identical prevalence in every culture, therefore my sister and I, together with all those good citizens who but fight a silent battle against the imperative of death on a daily basis, and there are many of us in this country, as is proved by the fact that three thousand five hundred people commit suicide every year in Spain, while for every suicide there are thirty attempts, I repeat, Julio, because I want this to be quite clear, for every person that voluntarily kills himself, there are thirty who try to do so, which gives us a figure of a hundred thousand, a hundred thousand Spaniards wanting to take their own lives every year, not a small

146

number, and this becomes even more frightening if we consider the fact there are a million suicides in the world every year, hence thirty million attempts during the same period, a number which is close to all the population of our country over the age of fourteen—close to almost all the population of Spain, Julio, the whole population!—a figure that should make us think we are faced by the largest epidemic of the twenty-first century, an epidemic that causes the death of many more people than AIDS, traffic accidents, homicides and military conflicts put together, and hence a plague that should make headlines every day in all the main newspapers, and yet it receives a tiny amount of attention in the press, basically because society doesn't want to hear about it, any journalist who dares cover the subject being labeled a pessimist, a defeatist or a nuisance, when in fact he should be awarded a monument to sincerity, all these statistics I've been telling you make it easier to understand why my sister and I have tried to take our own lives and will try again in the not too distant future, not because we've reached a philosophical conclusion about the meaninglessness of life, but because we have the same blood running through our veins, the polluted blood of those born with a faulty genetic code, blood that will always be resistant to any kind of psychological or pharmacological therapy, so I wouldn't bother too much trying to avoid the inevitable, Julio, because Elena is doomed to suffer and will end up taking her own life, however much you try to prevent it, she will make the most of the slightest occasion you become distracted, relax or simply get fed up, because you will get fed up, I'm telling you, you will get fed up of living in constant tension, and then you won't watch her with the same intensity, this is the absolute truth, my dear brother-in-law, the truth you will have to get used to, for in the end you will have to accept you can't do anything to fight against your wife's wishes, Julio, anything at all when confronted with the will-power of somebody who's taken a decision on the basis of an order issued by their genetic code. At this point, as I realize that some days ago Elena said something similar about not being able to keep an eye on her forever, Juan goes back to the toilet and, while he is sniffing another line of coke, I glance around to discover that all the customers in the bar are staring at our table, some with a pained expression etched in their faces, others on the verge of tears. This observation is interrupted when my brother-in-law returns and shows me a graph obviously designed by himself, with an ascending line reputedly showing an increase in the number of suicide attempts in this country over the last ten years, a decade during which the lust for death has rocketed, not because our living conditions are worse than they were a century ago, he goes on to say, but because there are more of us, there are many more human beings, and, since the carriers of this suicidal gene don't stop reproducing because the gene of suicide has yet to be activated inside them and they don't realize the harm they're doing to their children, since they don't stop screwing, as I was saying, they spread the seed of despair through their descendants, who will spawn in turn, multiplying their offspring, and so on, and so forth, in a continuum that will never cease, because the suicidal thought, the real suicidal thought, is not inside us from the beginning, it arises suddenly, when that fucking gene is activated and when in the spur of the moment we decide we're never going to tell anybody how our head is anchored to the idea of death, and, since nobody talks about it for fear of rejection, or rather almost nobody talks about it, because I'm talking about it right now, people are stunned whenever a friend or relative or colleague abruptly takes his own life, everybody exclaims, "But he seemed so normal!" They come out with this statement because they don't understand that normality, Julio, real normality, also includes people who want to die, or who don't want to live any more, depending on how you look at it, a normality that has become the most silent epidemic ever in the history of humanity, an epidemic that has spread all over the planet because humans tend to reproduce with great ease, an epidemic that is really quite similar to that of your mosquitoes, Julio, which will also spread more and more and more if you don't control them, in the same way the epidemic of suicides will propagate more and more and more widely if somebody doesn't do something about it, something right now, something before the day people with suicidal genes have managed to mix with all the population, the ones that enjoy life, that is, leading this plague to conquer the world to the extent where human beings will inevitably start jumping off balconies, bridges and buildings in every city in the world, and the children of those dead people will do the same, some time afterwards, as will the children of those dead people's children, and the children of those dead people's children's children, do you understand what I'm saying? All of them will jump off balconies, turning this and every town into a constant downpour of human beings, a flood of people whose only memory of happiness will occur during the seconds of their descent, a deluge of individuals relieved at the imminence of the death required by their genetic code for its fulfillment, and then, only then, when suicide has become the normal code of behavior in human beings, when this has become so obvious an official age is set after which committing suicide is considered positive, as it was in Viking culture, whose elders hanged themselves in the woods near Uppsala in order not to burden their communities, turning those woods into terribly dark places, when suicide has become normal and there are institutions to help people kill themselves, places you will go to ask for help with death, when this happens, Julio, when this really happens, science will have to accept that the theory concerning the genetics of voluntary death is not speculative, but proven, a proven fact that will have already become an epidemic, you see, an epidemic or even a pandemic so generalized hospitals will be set up where those wishing to die will be put to sleep by chemical means, as in euthanasia centers, there will be places you can go and say you can't cope with life any more, but don't have the balls to kill yourself, and in such circumstances the doctor will tell you not to worry, he can prescribe a drug that will increase the neurotransmitters that encourage self-injury and another chemical product that will reduce the amount of serotonin you may have left, in such a way that life will strike you as even more horrible, these doctors of death using medicines that make your brain even worse, and this will be the case because I don't think governments will accept public health services deliberately killing their patients, that would be murder, needless to say, and society will be hypocritical enough not to liquidate anyone who wants it, but to give them medicines that make them wish for death so badly not even cowardice will stop them from finding it, at which point everything will be sorted out, since taking one's own life will have become necessary in order not to continue suffering, something essential in order not to have to endure this pain for another second and not to cause suffering to those relatives responsible for our care, such as yourself, or my parents if I had told them that sometimes when I'm in the kitchen, I feel the urge to turn on the gas and send everything to hell, do you understand what I'm saying? Do you understand? You have to understand because I'm talking about the possibility of there being an anti-psychiatry movement one day, a real anti-psychiatry school, doctors who help you put an end to your suffering once and for all, instead of the psychiatry there is right now, which endeavors to help you overcome the negative ideas you were predestined to have as a human being. When my brother-in-law finishes his reasoning, if one could call it that, and seems to be swallowing marbles the size of footballs, everyone in the bar—the waiter, customers and I—has grown pale. Juan's voice has been getting louder as he expresses his opinions, and all those present, including a woman who has covered her ears with her hands in horror, remains silent, waiting for something to happen. Since I'm the one sitting opposite this sick man, I feel obliged to do something, so I slowly get to my feet, place my hands on the table and say as seriously as possible:

"Don't you ever dare set foot in my house again."

I drop a note on the table and head for the exit, not caring that Juan carries on staring in front of him, as if the chair opposite were still occupied, surrounded by his newspaper cuttings, in theory pondering the contents of his dissertation. He seems not to realize he's been left alone. That the world has turned its back on him. And now he's lost the chance to return to his sister's side to further his investigations, nobody is going to listen to his demented utterings. Not even me. Since I don't plan to endure for another second the ravings of a lunatic who thinks he's a scientist because he's read a couple of articles written by who knows who, I prepare to go out into the street and get the hell out of there, but I'm only a few feet from the door when the waiter stands in my way and pleads with me, even though nobody has asked him for his opinion, not to be so cruel, to which I reply, almost immediately, that he should mind his own business. At that moment, after I've dribbled past the busybody with the tray, a woman who happens to be the one that just covered up her ears in horror insists I should help this man because it's obvious he has lost his bearings, at which point somebody else, on this occasion a guy leaning against the bar, adds that only a son of a bitch would leave a poor devil like that one in such a lurch, and then a fourth individual accuses me of insensitivity, and then another customer adds his voice, followed by another, and so on, and so forth, until the whole bar, the whole disgusting, filthy bar, is hassling me to return to my seat and talk to a madman who, despite the good intentions shown by the present company, disappears to the toilet to snort another dose of lunacy. I am having to put up with half a dozen voices expressing their opinion regarding my behavior, three of whom go so far as to pat me on the back and encourage me to sit down at the table, without taking into account the fact that at this particular moment all I can think about is the open balcony of my house. And since it doesn't occur to them that I might be married to a woman whose mental health is at greater risk than that of my brother-in-law, I suddenly ask them, shouting like crazy, of course, what the hell do you think this is, hey, what the hell do you think this is, well, I'll tell you what it is: this is the suicidal brother of my equally suicidal wife, yes, that's right, you heard me, the suicidal brother of my similarly suicidal wife, a wife I will have to live with for the next ten years, who at this precise moment, while I'm here, wasting my time listening to your nonsense, is probably weighing up the advantages of jumping off the seventh floor where we live, and yet you, you bunch of busybodies, insist I should take care of a nutcase who can't stop snorting cocaine, a paranoiac who believes in the existence of an epidemic of suicides flooding the world, a moron, a half-wit who stuffs my head with ridiculous ideas about the importance of accepting the fact that my beloved wife, who happens to be the only woman I've ever loved and probably the only one who's ever loved me, is doomed to suffer for all eternity, and in circumstances like these you want me to look after him? Why don't you look after this jerk, hey, why don't you? Or rather, why don't you take a look around and finally accept you're living surrounded by the mentally ill, you're immersed in a society full of people who are depressed, anxious, schizophrenic, bipolar, unbalanced and I don't what else? Why don't you accept the fact we've invented a world covered in abysses? Why don't you face that fact, hey? Does it frighten you that much? Tell me. Are you so afraid you prefer to get drunk in order not to face the hostile environment? Does it terrify you so much, you damn cowards? Needless to say, after my rant they all lower their heads, most of them returning to their tables with their tail between their legs and one leaves the bar when he thinks no one is looking. I'm the one stalking them now, corralling them against their own consciences, while shouting you've got nothing to say now, have you, you disgusting hypocrites? You're so hypocritical you want me to look after this lunatic, but flee as soon as you're asked to help others. You make me sick, I hear myself saying, you really do. I corner the waiter behind the bar while asking him if he's ever wondered why his bar is full of loners at ten, eleven, twelve o'clock at night, have you? Have you ever stopped to think about it? You've never fucking thought about it, have you? You never have, nor will you, because you already know the answer, an answer you don't want to hear because you're terrified of hearing the truth, you couldn't bear owning up to the reason, the real reason this riff-raff spends its free time leaning on your counter, almost always in silence, like beings lost in the city, shadows fleeing from the light, souls awaiting the day they will finally be freed from their bodies, in short, living people who would rather be dead, desolate men and women searching for a smidgen of inner peace among the filth of this garbage deposit pretending to be a bar, every single one of your customers being incapable of enduring the solitude of their homes, needing a place to pretend they belong to something, they have somewhere to go, they haven't been completely rejected by society, so they come in here, into your shitty hole, and interact with a waiter who doesn't want to talk to them, who turns on the television to avoid listening to them, making sure he doesn't have to get involved in their lives, because deep down, you disgusting busybody, deep down you know perfectly well their lives are so pathetic, so utterly fucking pathetic, you don't want to get too close, you've enough on your plate with your awful routine to worry about others, right, you moron? Aren't I right? You have enough problems yourself to want to put up with the problems of this bunch of losers, isn't that so? At this point, feeling worn out by the effort of giving vent to all the anger built up inside me over the past week, if not the past year, I discover Juan standing in front of the door to the toilet, a half-smile on his lips, as if to say you see, Julito, deep down you and I agree. I walk out of the bar because otherwise I have the impression I will punch him on the nose and from the street I take one last look at the figure of my brother-in-law behind the window with the feeling I am never going to bump into this bum again. I sense tonight, having snorted another couple of lines and chucked I don't know what else down his throat, Juan will hang himself on the hook of the shower or turn on the gas in order, as he himself said, to send everything, parents included, to hell. The funniest thing is he may do this in the belief I, the only person with whom he has shared the secret fruits of his research, will comprehend the truth of his theory as soon as I learn of his demise. But he's wrong. Even if tomorrow he turns up stone dead in the bath-tub, even if he leaves a farewell note addressed to me, even if he sends all the cuttings he's accumulated over the years by mail, I won't waste a single second thinking about his death because I already have another human being to look after and I prefer to give my attention to a tiny mosquito rather than to a lunatic like him. To put it another way, I couldn't care less if he shot himself in front of the entrance to my building or threw himself under the wheels of my car. I don't give a damn. Really, I don't. The contempt I now feel for Juan is overwhelmingly superior to the sadness his death would cause me. Even so, as I pass by two beggars who don't even ask me for money and lift my eyes to see a billboard with a smiling young woman advertising toothpaste, I take my cellphone and ring the psychiatric emergency ward to give them the address of the bar.

I head home, thinking I should hire another babysitter before the morning, but, at this time of the night, I haven't a clue where to get hold of somebody willing to look after a woman with suicidal tendencies. I am pondering this question when I pass in front of a hardware store, and, despite the fact it's outside opening hours, I glimpse a light inside, at which point something creaks inside my brain, a sound slightly similar to that of a rusty hinge, which could be the hinge of the door giving access to the sewer of my spirit. Encouraged by this sudden illumination, I bang on the metal shutter of the shop, making such a racket the owner appears from behind the grille and scolds me for my behavior, an opportunity I use to plead with him to sell me a box of bolts, a drill and fifteen planks of wood. At first, the man doesn't seem prepared to serve me so early in the morning, but I only have to offer him four times the stipulated price for him to give me everything I want. He then helps me transport the material to the door of my building, where we put all the acquired objects in the elevator and I take my leave of a shopkeeper who, despite my unusual request, hasn't asked me a single question. I like people like him, by which I mean people who do what they have to do without demanding explanations, without sticking their nose in, without deviating from what's strictly professional. And yet, a second before getting out of my way forever, this man stares me in the eyes with disturbing intensity, as if he wished to examine the open trapdoor of my soul, and he says that sometimes, when it seems we're not going to find a solution to our problems, it's better to stand by and wait in the hope events will sort themselves out. He then leaves. Needless to say, I follow him because I want to ask him the real meaning of his words, but I only have to step on the sidewalk for another beam to rouse my senses, in this case a bolt of lightning announcing rain. I instinctively gaze at a partly overcast sky behind the cumuli of which I can make out a flickering light, which I imagine belongs to a plane, but I can't help seeing it as a message from the other side, a wink perhaps from the aperture of some storm cloud, a greeting maybe from my childhood neighbor who ended up breaking her spine on top of a mailbox and her face forever etched in my memory. When the first drop falls (maybe I should say the first tear), I feel a constriction in my chest, harbinger of an anxiety attack, which doesn't let me breathe. As the planet soaks my mien and the sky unburdens itself on my features, my face somehow becoming integrated in the cycle of nature repeated over millions and millions and millions of years, I have the impression all pain, absolutely all the pain in this world, has landed on my conscience and, turning my attention toward the building opposite, a fifteen-floor colossus with about a hundred people inside watching the same programs on TV and sleeping on mattresses of the same brand, I start thinking we human beings have created a society that is so ordered, so brutally geometrical, it doesn't resemble the individuals, chaotic individuals, who make it up. My wife wants to die because she can't find a way to place herself in this grid called reality, and I, a man who is perfectly adapted to the city's demands, a worker who is aware that only men of action, not passive ones, prosper in this life, have decided not to let her die by transforming my apartment into a fortress, a prison, if you like, which no one will be able to gain access to and from which, more importantly, no one will be able to escape. I have bought fifteen wood slats because I intend to shut Elena in, so I confront my demons by taking a deep breath and returning to the building, climbing into the elevator and entering my home, where I carry all the material I've bought to the living room and, not caring that my wife is watching me, I close the door to the balcony, drill holes in the wall and bar the door with two of the planks placed sideways. During the hours that follow, I carry on nailing planks to the windows of the bedroom, the toilet, the kitchen, as I am convinced that the only way to keep my wife at my side is to lock her in. While I perform such operations, Elena wanders about the house, watching what I'm up to. But she doesn't intervene. Nor does she speak. She doesn't even look surprised. She simply remains silent, as she has done ever since she swallowed that blister pack of sleeping pills, until at a certain point she retires to the bedroom and doesn't reappear for the whole night, not even when I hammer away at a plank or when I kick the walls of the "creepy-crawly room", a room that strikes me now, at least in my subconscious, as the source of all our ills. Finally, when no exit has been left unbarred, I stare at the fruit of my labors, which is none other than the construction of a perfect cage, almost as perfect as any of the traps I set in the gardens of the town where I'm trying to capture the tiger mosquito, and I've sat down to rest for a while when, around six in the morning, my laboratory assistant calls me with the news she's just captured a specimen of *Aedes albopictus*. Needless to say, I am overwhelmed with anger. I have dreamed of being the first scientist in this country to lay eyes on such for years, but Nuria, an intern who hasn't even graduated, has got ahead of me because I was unable to fulfill the responsibilities entrusted to me. That is why right at this moment, I feel a terrible need to beat up somebody. Anybody. This urge increases when I glimpse the face of my wife peeping out from behind the door of the bedroom, apparently willing to tell me something, perhaps to reveal once and for all what's been going on inside her brain. And yet, when she comes across my face twisted with resentment, she withdraws into the shadows of the bedroom in a way which is incredibly similar to the manner in which the widow from apartment number two vanishes every time I catch her spying on me from her balcony. Instead of pleading with her to share with me what she wanted to say, I grab her set of keys, go out on to the landing, yank the telephone cable from the wall and lock the door from the outside. I then lean against the wall for a few seconds. I stare at the ceiling, my breathing labored, the neighbor's eye pressed against the peephole. I imagine my wife coming out of our bedroom. Walking around a house that has been turned into a prison. Wandering down the corridor in the shape of a cross. And a voice inside me whispers you've shut your wife in, Julito, you've shut your wife in.

6

I am driving down the highway at top speed, as if I were taking part in a time trial and death were at my heels, while casting glances at the case containing the *Aedes albopictus specimen*. Insects crash into the windshield, a couple of inches away from the dashboard on which I have placed my prey, and there's nothing I can do to prevent it, on the contrary, I accelerate a little more with the idea my mosquito might be able to see its peers getting squashed against the glass, in the same way my neighbor smashed into the mailbox and hundreds of human beings, at this precise moment, are surely crashing against the sidewalk of their streets, their cities, their lives, in short. Less than a week ago, having locked my wife inside the house, I returned to the town where Nuria was waiting with the first specimen ever captured in this country and no sooner had I got out of the car than I seized the cage, removed the dipteran and, having observed for a couple of seconds what was undoubtedly a perfect specimen, I crushed it between my fingers. My assistant couldn't believe her eyes. She couldn't understand what would make me behave in this way, so she started screaming, demanding an explanation and getting fired as a result, at which she threatened to report me to the dean, to the National Association of Entomologists, to the Minister of the Environment even, and in reply I suggested she should do whatever she liked. Then I turned around and left. Over the following hours, I dismantled all the traps she'd set up—keen as I was to reach my goal without anybody's help—and placed some new ones in the exact same places where the others had been. And I waited. After five days, I discovered a mosquito in one of the cases and congratulated myself on having captured the first verifiable specimen of *Aedes albopictus*. Obviously, there was no one for me to share my joy with, so I limited myself to quaffing several beers in a local bar, toasting myself in the mirror of the toilet and informing the waiter, to whom I left a remarkably generous tip, by the way, that he was in the presence of an extraordinary scientist, a statement that didn't seem to pique his interest even when I placed the case on top of the bar, showed him the insect and explained I had shed blood, sweat and tears to capture this specimen, an effort that had become increasingly tiring as the days went by, one, two, three, four, five—it's no mean feat spending five days in this shitty little town, you know, while constantly keeping an eye on the second hand of my watch, suffering every time it advanced, knowing my wife was still shut away and, by this time, had probably ransacked every drawer in the house in search of an implement that would put an end to her physical or psychical imprisonment, it doesn't matter which, you see, though I must admit I suspect my wife would prefer to put an end to the second rather than the first, by which I mean Elena would pay even to end her life rather than her captivity. I explained all this to the bar owner, who showed not the slightest interest in what I had to say or in the dipteran buzzing on top of the counter, at least not until I ordered my eighth beer, at which point he stopped drying the glasses with a filthy rag he kept hanging on his shoulder and informed me I had drunk enough and it was time I returned to the city. Barely half an hour later, I am driving down the highway at top speed, the case on top of the dashboard and my foot on the accelerator, while recalling how over the last five days, as I checked the traps positioned in every corner of this municipality, I often thought about my wife weeping on the sofa cushions or banging the front door, hoping the neighbor would come to her rescue, or hurting her hands after scraping the boards that cover a window whose appearance is very similar to that of the methacrylate covering the case with my specimen, which makes me think what I'm transporting is not really a mosquito, but a miniature version of my wife, with whom I haven't been able to communicate once, since I pulled out the telephone cable to stop her using it as a noose. I remember how during these last few days I have been haunted by an even more depressing image of my wife lying in the middle of the corridor, where the cross in our apartment is formed, her arms extended at the point of intersection, and, after this vision, I felt a need to talk to her, a need that couldn't be fulfilled, but which kept on gnawing at me until in the end it turned into a nightmare repeated over five nights, a bad dream in which I awoke in the middle of a wood full of nooses swaying in the wind, waiting for bodies to tighten them, and my wife in the background, standing on a heap of fallen leaves, searching for a branch to put an end to her suffering, a rope to remove her from this world, a knot she suddenly discovers on a tree, an ancient oak she climbs while staring at the camera that is me, in an attempt to take her leave, it seems, as a way of saying see you later, Julito. Then she falls. First, the crunch of her neck. Then, her feet hanging in the air. Finally, the urine in her trousers. Before waking, I take one last look at the grove of trees that has turned into a gloomy place and glimpse several faces agonizing inside the trunks, like bas-reliefs sculptured in the tree bark, probably souls writhing in that wood of suicides where, according to tradition, all those who raised a hand against themselves suffer forever.

On finally entering the city, I realize that, while I'm in a hurry to get home, I'm not driving in the right direction, but heading somewhere else, judging by the signs pointing northward, perhaps the area I grew up in, and I discover my mind has focused on a single idea, an impulse, pushing me toward the place where I turned into a little boy always looking inward. In spite of desperately forcing myself not to, I drive toward the past, and my hands, which seem no longer to belong to me, turn the steering wheel first right, then left and finally toward the building of my childhood, where my darkest memories reside, into the heart of my own darkness. I want to go forward, never backward, not only because it's essential I release Elena from her captivity, but also because I must place the dipteran in another container, a nursery equipped for its survival, since I cannot allow myself the luxury of mistreating, and hence killing, the first tiger mosquito to be captured in this country alive. And yet I can't get my other self— that is the one still feeling the urge of the past—to turn toward the future, so I enter the district where I endured that awful childhood and reach the building in front of which is the same mailbox on which that woman split her head open. I park opposite the shop that used to be the baker's where I called my mother a liar, go inside a building coated in flaking paint, climb the stairs, refusing to use the elevator where I once wet myself, and reach the fourth floor, where memories flood me like beams of light. Before pressing my old neighbors' doorbell, I gaze at the door opposite, the door behind which my parents still don't understand what caused me to break off all relations as soon as I became independent, a door that is really a gateway to the past. It suddenly occurs to me that perhaps the time of reconciliation has come, time to return to a maternal bosom that would surely accept me with open arms, this possibly being the ideal opportunity to admit to my progenitors that my life has derailed, my present life never formed part of my plans and I have great, enormous difficulties regaining control of my future. For a short while, I weigh up the advantages of building a bridge between us, of going back to a couple of seconds prior to the moment the neighbor believed she was an angel, but reject this option when I remember my mother's determination to transmute reality, an inclination that may still form part of her character, which will make her end up trying to console me by hinting that Elena maybe did not want to commit suicide, but to have a little siesta inside the closet, and I'm the one distorting the facts by continuing to believe, as I did in my childhood, that there's something so repugnant in me everybody would rather die than be in my company, arguments my mother will come out with so naturally I may even take them into consideration for a second, but will immediately refute because they sound like nonsense and then, it goes without saying, I will call my mother a fucking liar, a filthy hag, a repressed bitch, and she in turn will censure my vocabulary and give me a clip around the ear to make me learn, once and for all, that if she says a pig can fly, it's because a pig really can fly. And since I'm not in the mood to put up with alterations of reality or to receive treacherous slaps in the face, I turn my back on the house where I grew up and press the bell of the door opposite, at which Manolo shows his face, his old decrepit face and asks me what I want.

He doesn't recognize me, and I don't explain who I am. I just stare at him in the hope he will discover in my eyes the child there was once inside me, but, instead of delving into his memories, Manolo, no doubt frightened by my attitude and thinking I'm a criminal, tries to shut the door so unsuccessfully I jam it with my foot and, before he can cry out for help, I slip into his hall, cover his mouth and bolt the door behind me. I then order him not to shout and only take my hand away when he nods in agreement. After that, I tell him it's Julito, Julito Garrido, your old neighbor. I realize he's recognized me because his expression suddenly changes, he leans back and slides down the wall until he ends up sitting on a trunk where he covers his face and, through a mixture of snot, trembles and whines, pleads for forgiveness with the same intensity as on that evening in the elevator. Fortunately, I'm no longer a child, I can control my wish to pee, so I tell him to calm down and enter a house that stinks to high heaven, a house full of dust, cigarette butts and grime, a house that is clearly marked by suffering. In the dining room, I come across a table with two plates, one dirty and the other clean, which makes me think Manolo planned to have supper with somebody who didn't turn up, I imagine his deceased wife, and, on the back of the sofa, I detect a shawl, which I suppose is the one his wife wore when they used to watch television so many years ago. After that, I enter the bedroom, where I find a photo album on one of the pillows, no doubt containing portraits of their wedding, trips, parties, in short all the happy moments of their marriage, and where I also discover, on the right of the mattress, a pair of slippers with a floral design that must have been there for more than twenty years. Then, while noticing two toothbrushes lying on a shelf in the bathroom, one of which is in a filthy state, I am reminded of an experiment carried out by a group of entomologists at my university. Over several weeks, they reared a couple of insects—coleopterans, if I remember rightly—in an enclosed environment, so they only had each other for company. One of the specimens, the female, was painted with a white spot on its outer shell, I suppose to make the male remember it more easily, and, after a period of time, once the insects had consolidated their relationship and accepted each other, the researchers eliminated the specimen with the spot, leaving its partner in the most absolute solitude for three days, at which point they introduced into the terrarium a blackish stone of similar dimensions to those of the dead beetle, a pebble painted with a white dot where its back was supposed to be and rubbed with the previous insect's corpse, so it would be impregnated with its smell. As all the students were able to observe, no sooner had the pebble been placed in the box than the male went up to it, seemingly oblivious to the change that had taken place, and, from that moment onward, spent hours in the company of an object that, however inanimate it may have been, reminded it of its old partner. Shortly afterwards, the entomologists placed other animals of the same species in the case with the aim of checking whether the coleopteran would abandon the stone in favor of a more active female and confirmed that the specimen preferred to remain next to the entelechy with the white spot, to which it brought food from time to time and which it cuddled up to for warmth on artificial laboratory nights, showing quite clearly it had no intention of rebuilding its life. At the end of its life, after substances that were harmful to its health had been administered to speed up its vital processes, the insect lay down beside the beloved object of its memories and gave itself up to death without having paid the slightest attention to the other insects that tried to establish a relationship and even attacking any creature that approached the stone impregnated with its ex-partner's aromas. The experiment didn't end there. The scientists, keen to further their research and I suspect enjoying the suffering inflicted on those animals, repeated the exercise with other individuals of the same species, verifying that most would enter into new relations with any females that appeared in the terrarium after the disappearance of their first mate, while a small minority—one in every fifty, as I remember—would reject the new arrivals and somehow remain faithful to the pebble, and there even being the case of a beetle which, when the stone he constantly showered with affection was taken away, carried on spurning the other tenants in honor of the empty space occupied by its partner before it suddenly vanished. I remember vividly how, after a period of time, the girls in my class stopped coming to the laboratory, appalled by the cruelty of the scene, although they may also have been uncomfortable because of the paradox of witnessing such displays of tenderness in such a disgusting creature. But the most curious thing about the whole affair, or at least what surprised me most, was the way the male students showed absolutely no interest in their defection, going so far as to make jokes about the girls' susceptibility to the suffering of others, when in truth I think what was most interesting about those days was precisely our reaction, by which I mean I've always thought we were the real experiment and the terrarium with the beetles was just the bait placed by some invisible scientists to draw us to that room and calmly study our reactions, so they could confirm the way males of the human species boasted about being more impervious to others' suffering than females, while all we did, poor idiots, was laugh at a coleopteran that only wanted a bit of company. Be that as it may, as I recall those afternoons in front of a terrarium in which a beetle revealed to us what could be considered the immensity of love, I think Manolo belongs to the category of insects lacking the requisite mental attributes to understand it's necessary to rebuild one's life after the loss of a loved one, and it flashes across my mind that this apartment, this building, this city even, is nothing more than a huge terrarium whose glass walls conceal a great scientist I don't mind calling God, who never ceases to be amazed by the absurdity of our reactions, such as putting an empty plate on the table, or laying a dusty shawl on the back of the sofa, or keeping some floral slippers on the right side of the bed, and a bunch of other details that, in the case we are examining, go to show quite clearly that, twenty years or so after her death, this poor devil continues to pretend his little beetle is still alive, nothing has changed since his wife committed suicide and the house smells the same as when she was in it, which is plainly false. I am aware this old man represents what I could become, should Elena definitively take her own life, and this frightens me so much that, afraid I might be seeing my own future reflected in this individual's present, I decide to beat it. I am just about to leave the apartment when the widower bursts out laughing. He suddenly lets out a guffaw, the way a raving lunatic would, and, since I fail to understand what he finds so funny, I ask him what's going on. He doesn't reply. He just goes on laughing and laughing and laughing without paying any attention to me, so I grab him by the lapels, yank him to his feet and demand he calm down. But he carries on splitting his sides so theatrically that I can't hold back and I slap him hard, then I hit him again and, since he doesn't stop cracking up, I punch him so hard I break his nasal septum. Covering his now bloody face, he suppresses his laughter and repeatedly assures me he's in no position to help me, I won't find what I'm looking for in his apartment and I've wasted my time by trying to find it here. At no moment have I said what the motive of my visit is, but he doesn't seem to need any explanations and he surprises me by saying I will never manage to clear up the events I witnessed on the afternoon of my childhood and the mailbox, since he's been trying to do the same for the last twenty-five years. He then sheds a few tears and tells me he misses his wife, he really misses her, you've no idea how much I miss her, Julito, you've no idea.

"My wife also wants to commit suicide," I confess eventually.

" …"

"And I don't know how to stop her."

" …"

"I thought you might have some answers."

"Well, you were wrong."

There's a photograph that doesn't stop looking at me, a picture of his wife smiling broadly and the sky in the background, the same sky from which she must now be spying on us, a sky where pain does not exist, a sky that, needless to say, is immeasurably empty.

"Did you know your wife was thinking about committing suicide?" I ask.

"She never told me, but these things are obvious."

"Didn't you do anything about it?"

"What could I do?"

"Stop her."

"You can't do that."

"I locked my wife away. To keep her by my side."

He twists his neck to where I'm standing, revealing the blood stains on his face.

"That's not going to keep her by your side. Probably the opposite."

I head for the exit, since I've understood this guy isn't going to help me, he is stuck in the past and has nothing to offer.

171

"I'm very sorry about all the pain my wife's death may have caused you," he says. "She shouldn't have jumped when you were on the other balcony. No, she really shouldn't."

He holds me back again with these words:

"She was very fond of you, you know. She always used to talk about you. How handsome you were. How clever. How nice."

"Well, she changed all of that."

"She didn't mean to."

This answer is not enough.

"My wife needed to die and couldn't wait another second," he goes on. "Some people are like that. People who can't put up with reality. People who abandon us because they can't continue living in this world. People like my wife … People like yours …"

When I've opened the front door, Manolo takes the portrait of the dead woman with a backdrop of sky, caresses the face printed behind the glass and mutters the following:

"At least you can say goodbye to her. My wife jumped unexpectedly. I knew she was going to do something bad, but I didn't know when. One day, she was no longer there. If you have the chance to say goodbye to her, don't let it go to waste. Tell her you love her. And then give her the freedom she needs."

"I don't know if I'll be able to do that."

"You won't be able to stop her either."

I am on the landing when he grabs me by the arm, preventing me from moving away, and opens his heart:

"Don't leave."

"I have to."

"Please don't."

"Let go of me."

"Stay a little longer. Just a little."

"Let go of me, I said!"

I manage to free my arm from his grasp. Manolo stands, leaning against the door-jamb, his face still bleeding, watching me from the darkest dungeon inside his brain, a mere inhabitant of the black castle of loneliness.

"Don't leave," I hear him in the distance. "Stay a little. Just a little."

After exiting the building, I settle into my car with the intention of writing a letter to my parents in which I confess to them straight out, without bothering with greetings, that I miss them and where I recognize that, despite our misunderstandings, I still love them. I then buy an envelope and a stamp, cross the street and, although I'm near their house and so could deliver it by hand, I head toward the mailbox, the same mailbox on which the woman who has become a childhood memory spilled her brains. Before posting the missive, I raise my eyes to the balcony of the fourth floor where I grew up, possibly wanting Julito's head—my own head, therefore—to show itself and look at me from that physical distance which is also temporal distance, and I'm standing like this when I think there's something rather poetic in the fact of using the same mailbox to communicate to my parents that, so many years after the event that distanced me from them, I still need them. On dropping the envelope into the yellow mouth that strikes me now as the self-same entrance to hell—by which I mean I imagine the inside of this contraption like a large well which runs under the pavement and descends down a cold, dark, narrow tunnel until it reaches a crypt that may be even more cramped than my "creepy-crawly room", a dungeon in which my soul has resided for some time and where there are no doors or windows or cat-flaps or hatches, or anything at all except for me, this pitiful, ridiculous, absurd being—when I finally drop the envelope into the mouth of this place, as I was saying, and when in turn I watch it with the eyes of my imagination hurtling down that well, a shiver runs down my spine, a trembling that shakes the malodorous vault under which my soul writhes in agony and helps me understand the letter I've just sent is reminiscent of a farewell. Before placing this note in the mailbox, it hadn't occurred to me that my words might be concealing not only the desire to make up with those who brought me into this world, but also the need to exonerate them of everything that has happened in recent years and, more importantly, of everything that is going to happen in the coming days. And yet, at this precise moment, as I stare at the railing of my old house—where by the way I'm still waiting for a child to appear so I can tell him to go back inside his apartment, saving him from witnessing his neighbor's suicide and so preventing him from having a future marked by a deep fear of abandonment—at this precise moment, I think placing this letter inside the selfsame mailbox that woman smashed into is no more than a way of proclaiming my decision to embark on a road of no return, to enter a cave leading straight to the land no one ever comes back from, and I won't either. I wrote these words after finding out that Manolo has spent decades eating next to the empty chair his wife used to sit on, settling down into a sofa where he is accompanied only by a shawl and sleeping on a bed at the foot of which he has placed a dead woman's slippers, all attitudes that make me afraid, among many other things, that my parents might have kept my bedroom as I left it and sometimes, when they are overwhelmed by nostalgia, they may go into this room to recover, albeit for only a few seconds, their hope in a world where the young don't abandon their elders, where children don't have to confront horror too early, where life isn't a battle against the monsters, implacable monsters, that devour the plate on which we were served a starter of happiness. Witnessing my old neighbor's madness has made me think my parents might be living my absence with the same intensity as the widower, since at this stage in my story I have learned there isn't much difference between committing suicide and abandoning someone, between leaving and fleeing, between not being and not wanting to be. And that is why right now all I want is for my progenitors to know how to interpret the message I'm sending them with this letter and to be able to appreciate the fact I am taking my leave by asking their forgiveness for so many years of emptiness.

Having settled these matters and driven around the lonely corners of the city, which strike me as remarkably similar to the loneliness of the man who dines with a shadow from his past, I arrive at my building, where for the first time I don't have the feeling all the peepholes have turned into eyes and where, also for the first time, I think that, having reached this point of no return, I couldn't give a damn if my neighbors spy on my movements, since at present I consider myself far removed from their petty concerns. I don't even glance at the door of apartment two on the seventh floor, right now I don't even feel contempt for its owner, and enter my apartment in the shape of a cross, where I turn on the light, alarmed by the darkness into which it has been subsumed. There's nobody in the corridor. Nothing but silence. And, at the far end, the door to the living room waiting to be opened. I gaze at it from a distance, and everything inside my head becomes mixed up, leading me to believe I'm not in the corridor of my house, but in the devil's throat, at the bottom of which is the closed pit of a stomach where hundreds of souls sentenced to eternal suffering squirm in agony. I even have the impression everything is moving, as if the monster had started to swallow, when in fact I know this agitation stems from the vertigo caused by my anxiety. I try to calm myself down by placing my hands on both walls and taking a deep breath while getting ready to meet whatever lies on the other side. I slowly gather my senses, but remain next to the front door for a few seconds because the stillness in this house reminds me of the day my wife sought the confines of the closet and then, when I notice it's the same time it was on the night when everything started, I seriously begin to consider the possibility that a superior being, a paranormal phenomenon, has brought me back to the origin of this story. I am bewildered at the sight of this corridor I've been down so often, a corridor that suddenly strikes me as a sort of time machine transporting me irrevocably toward the past, a situation that becomes so vivid in my mind that for a moment I'm a step away from repeating the actions I carried out on that accursed day.

So I think about shouting, as I shouted on that occasion, darling I'm home, and I also remember, as I recalled back then, how my wife doesn't like me to hang up my coat by myself, and after that I imagine searching for the hiding place where she must have concealed herself in order to celebrate our fifth wedding anniversary, and then asking the widow from apartment number two if my wife is there, and also running down the stairs, having found her cellphone in the garbage, and squatting on the pavement looking for remains of entrails on the concrete, and in the end returning to a house where I open the doors to the closet, discover the almost lifeless body of Elena and regret the moment I ever complained about not being the object of a surprise party. I suppose I torment myself with such fantasies because, in the bottom of my heart, I think the sins committed in the past few days, by which I mean the imprisonment I've subjected my wife to for almost a week, deserve some time in the hell of eternal recurrence, but I immediately decide the devil doesn't need to sentence me to reliving these events for ever and ever because the psychiatrist with button eyes already did that when he announced that for the next ten years, no more and no less than each and every damn day that will make up the next ten years, I would have to live with the fear of my wife again trying to take her own life. So there's no difference between repeating the past and confronting the future because in both cases I will have to face a corridor each evening where pain awaits behind the door.

On finally entering the living room and confirming that my wife is not there, I glimpse the windows of the building opposite, the owners of which have lowered their blinds, probably to avoid the feeling of claustrophobia caused by the shadows of planks projected on to their façade, shadows that have covered their windows for five nights, making them think, subliminally perhaps, they also inhabit a prison from where they will never escape, a prison they may call "city", perhaps "work" or possibly "marriage", it doesn't really matter. Although it could also be true they lowered their blinds to lose sight of the woman on the balcony of the seventh floor opposite their homes, who has spent the last five nights peeping out from between the planks, staring at them with absent eyes and tormenting their resting hours with her appearance of hopelessness. When I realize how these people have turned their back on my wife, drawing the curtains with the same cowardice as when we pretended not to hear the neighbor on the fourth floor beating his spouse, I deduce that the busybodies of this district—and, in truth, of any other—stop gossiping as soon as they are invited to get involved in somebody else's problems. My situation no longer causes me vertigo, but a deep-seated disgust of the human condition, or rather of the urban condition. Fed up of so much truth, I take a few steps backward, intending to search for Elena in another room, but, on turning around, still thinking about the cowardice of humankind, I glimpse her figure curled up in the angle of the door, and I don't need to observe her appearance in any great detail to conclude she's been in this nook for a long time. My wife must have settled in this place soon after I abandoned her, and for five days she has remained in the same position, probably without washing or eating, waiting for me to return. I suppose so many nights squashed into this cranny have destroyed her joints, as well as the edges of her soul, because right now, as I lean forward to caress her face, she shrinks away from me, like a child afraid of a beating, and begs me not to touch her. Then, when she seems to have calmed down and allows me to lift her chin with my hand, I unveil a face which doesn't denote suffering, but the most inaccessible madness. Luckily, after having stared at me for a while with unsettling intensity, she seems to recognize me. But she doesn't slap me, or call me selfish, or even spit in my face. Nor does she beg me never to abandon her again. She remains in her corner, waiting for me to let go of her face so she can sink it between her legs and plunge again into a mind that has turned into a labyrinth. And at that moment I am glad to have nailed planks all over the house. Because finding my wife in such a state makes me consider myself so disgusting, so revoltingly disgusting, I wouldn't mind annihilating myself by leaping into the void. But I can't do it, so I limit myself to standing in front of the balcony, grasping two of the boards and, having taken a lungful of air, letting out a scream, probably the most terrifying scream in history, a scream that is capable of freezing in mid air the fall of all those human beings that have just jumped off the balconies, cliffs and terrace roofs anywhere on this planet. As my scream is prolonged, I imagine the skydivers of the entire world suspended a few inches above the ground, turning their heads to the heights, to a point above the ledges they used as trampolines, regretting an act they committed in a moment of bewilderment, something that causes them to ask someone up there for a second chance, as if they've abruptly understood that the jump they've just performed, this jump that will carry them deathward, has served only to deprive them of the happiness life had in store for them, or they've finally comprehended, once and for all, the great truth all suicides of the world should aspire to, a truth the rest of us mortals took on board in our earliest childhood, but some people fail to elaborate, which is that nobody can be unhappy forever. At this precise moment, as the lack of gravity enables them for a few seconds to contemplate the obvious beauty of this world and experience the pleasure of the wind caressing their eyelashes and the grandeur of human achievement as exemplified by light-filled cities, all these divers pray the heavens above to grant them the miracle of wings. The apterous angels hanging above the ground ask the heights for some appendages that will allow them to regain the balconies, cliffs, terrace roofs, they first jumped off and in their head hear the same words the psychiatrist who attended Elena said to me, by which I mean that all failed suicides, absolutely all of them, regret their attempt immediately after they've carried it out, which would indicate that, in the seconds a fall lasts or the minutes a body needs to bleed to death, those who don't fail also repent of finding themselves in such a situation on account of a run of bad luck. I can easily imagine the remorse of those who've just thrown themselves out of the window, their wish to turn back the clock a few seconds, to just before the moment they got carried away, a desire that will end as soon as they crash on the sidewalk, as happens with the longings of all those who've remained in suspension on account of my scream, a scream that inevitably turns into an echo, an echo condemned to silence which, when it finally peters out, will sentence the poor wretches floating for a few moments—those who understood the beauty of this world for the milliseconds they were allowed to float or believe they were floating—to croak on the ground. Their impact on the sidewalk creates such a din inside my head that right now, as I collapse on the parquet, musing on how wonderful it would be to possess the power to grant a second chance to all those who never stopped to think that every leap into the void is necessarily definitive, as I realize I would sacrifice my own life to give back life to all those individuals who made such a blatant mistake, as I plead with God to let all mortals comprehend that suffering has an expiry date and they only have to wait another day, a second day if necessary, and a third, and so on, until the pain in their soul goes away, having thought about all this, I hear inside me the crunch of their skulls shattering on the concrete. I burst into tears, full of despair, causing Elena to drag herself across the floor to where I am, stroke the back of my neck and murmur my name. When I discern the infinite tenderness in her voice, I believe in the possibility of redemption, so I show her my face, hold out my hand and, seeing she lets me, I embrace her with such strength I think I could pass straight through her body to the other side. After a while, when I muster up the courage to ask if she's still obsessed with death, she puts a finger to my lips, begging me not to spoil the moment with words, and tells me to show her the case with the tiger mosquito I've been after for such a long time. But my head can't stop, and it occurs to me that showing her this insect will create a kind of end-game between us. By which I mean, when she understands that the effort of recent years has reached its culmination, when she contemplates the dipteran I've struggled so much to lay my hands on, when she sees it in a cage somewhat similar to the prison I've turned our apartment into, she will say there's no reason for us to continue in this world. She may suggest that, like her, I've always thought about suicide as a solution to my disagreement with life and, when she's implied she knows my fears better than I do—she's perfectly aware that ever since my earliest childhood, in particular ever since I witnessed my neighbor's fall, I've always considered the possibility of blowing my brains out—when she makes this patent, I will confess I've never known happiness, but am still among the living because I have her, she is the only joy in my life, and need to keep her by my side so that life doesn't become something it's no longer worth fighting for. I've never directly confessed to her that she's my only anchorage in this world, nor do I dare say this right now, basically because I'm afraid she'll reject my words. So I allow myself to be pulled along to the "creepy-crawly room", picking up the case with the tiger mosquito specimen along the way, and, when I open the door to my study, I discover the walls are covered in photographs. During the last five days, apart from lying curled up in a ball in the corner of the living room, my wife has taken apart the photo albums from her childhood, youth and adulthood in order to turn my refuge into a mirror of her existence and, when I take a step forward, attracted by the scene that meets my eyes, I hear from my wife's lips a sentence that doesn't surprise me in the slightest:

"I don't know why I want to die, but I can't stop wishing it."

I contemplate the photographs affixed to the walls of this room and notice she's also taken apart the albums from my childhood, youth and adulthood, alternating her images with my own in what appears to be an attempt to remind me that we are one, for better, for worse, for richer, for poorer, in sickness and in health, most of all in sickness and in health, and will never be able to separate our stories, even when death comes to claim one of us. As I pay closer attention, I realize that, in the middle of the photographs, there is one of me as a boy where I appear next to the neighbor of my childhood, which just goes to show I can't separate my story from this woman and, to some extent, nobody can ever cut themselves off from the individuals who've had a strong influence on their lives. The picture was taken on the balcony of our house, I suppose during one of those afternoons when my parents, wanting to maintain good relations with the other tenants, invited them to have tea at home. In the image, I am sitting on the lap of this lady who in a not too distant future would say see you later, Julito, somebody who seems now to have a strange look in her eyes, I would even dare to say a suicidal look, an interpretation that may well be derived from the knowledge I currently have about her, by which I mean the certainty she'd end up jumping off the balcony, which makes me scrutinize her face in search of something in her eyes, something that denotes inner suffering, something I wouldn't be looking for if I wasn't aware what she was going to end up doing. The photo is in the center of one of the walls, next to another one showing Elena with a smile, where I also try to find something in her eyes as a result of the information

I possess about her mental health. It's a portrait taken a couple of years ago, before she'd fallen into a depression, or at least before the depression had been diagnosed. I compare one photo with the other, searching for similar features, a clue to help me understand them, a gesture that classifies them in the same group. But I can't find anything. And then I spot a third image above these two, showing me without a smile, a distracted look in my eyes, and I realize I'm the only link between these two women, uniting their actions at least, which means I'm the one who has to make a difference between the former's final days and the latter's next ten years. In an attempt to divert my attention from such reflections, I invite Elena to admire with me the first living specimen of a tiger mosquito in captivity and, having gazed at it with delight, with so much delight she frightens me, she declares she feels the same as this insect. So I take my wife by the hand, the dipteran's box in the other, and we head to the living room, where we sit on the sofa. I leave the case on the table and open the trapdoor. I then rest my head in my wife's lap without her offering any resistance. We don't say anything. We don't move. We don't even look into each other's eyes. I only have eyes for the ceiling because I'm waiting for the mosquito to appear at any moment and, while waiting for this to happen, I remember situations experienced on this sofa, as when we enjoyed some film or she fell asleep, hugging a cushion, and immediately conclude Elena was right when she said, in the shop where we had our wedding list, we would spend many happy hours on this sofa. Until recently, I was of the opinion nothing particularly noteworthy had ever happened on this piece of furniture, but now I understand the chats we had in front of the television, even the lack of chats in front of the television, as well as the days when I read while she drew or she drank coffee while I watched her, were happy moments. It's a shame it's taken me so long to realize this. Because there's no going back any more. I've taken the decision to become the distinguishing factor between my neighbor's suicide and my wife's, and it's not possible to recover the past. Besides, freeing the dipteran, in an odd sort of way, symbolizes the destruction of all our dreams, dreams that are finally fluttering next to the light, dreams for an apartment with an entrance hall, a future full of kids, a peaceful life. The point is I no longer care about becoming a first-rate scientist, if I can't do it with Elena at my side. My despair is so great all I wish for now is for this mosquito to reproduce and for the colony it will soon create in this city to flourish. In fact, I'm so full of confidence about the capacity of this insect to populate the local municipality that, perhaps for the first time in my life, I feel frankly proud of myself. Because I've introduced a new element into this country's habitat, and by doing so I've made reality more diverse.

After a while, I stand up in order to unblock the door to the terrace and let the mosquito pounce on the city. I know I'm unleashing a plague worth twenty-five million euros. But I don't care. I feel a need to take revenge on society because I'm of the opinion that all, absolutely all of its members, have contributed to the failure of my expectations, together with those of my wife, by keeping silent regarding our misfortunes. Hundreds of individuals take their own life throwing themselves on to the subway tracks, jumping from the heights of their balconies, in the bathrooms of their homes, among the branches of their woods, in so many different places, while others stuff themselves full of anti-depressants, sedatives and sundry anti-psychotics. But nobody says anything about it. Nobody is prepared to confront this reality, and my wife suffers because she has no one to share her dismal thoughts with. So right now, as the mosquito buzzes next to the window, I recall my brother-in-law's words when he said voluntary deaths would turn into a pandemic of biblical proportions, and for a moment I deduce that the real plague, the one that can no longer be stopped, is called fear. A fear that makes people fall silent. That triumphs over our silence. That crushes us. If we all confessed our inner fears, if we talked about our plans to harm ourselves, suicide would turn into a reality accepted by everybody and so be easier to fight, just like the tiger mosquito's colonization if detected in time. But people keep quiet, and suicides have fantasies. They feel lonely, they think they've been abandoned, they see themselves as different, when in truth their act is one of the most common acts performed by human beings. Because of this, when I think my tiger mosquito will make these cowards' lives a little less comfortable, I laugh to myself. This is my revenge. My liberation, if you like. Who knows? I watch the dipteran flying on to the balcony and catch sight of the dog opposite. The mutt stares at us for a few seconds, then pricks up its ears and suddenly emits such an agonizing howl that I—and my wife as well, I suppose—understand this story has come to an end. We take the car keys and, before leaving for our destination—the only destination possible—wander about the house in a vain attempt to recapture happy memories. As we walk out of each room, we close the door until, at the end of our journey, by the time we're at the foot of the cross, the future has become a corridor of sealed doors. The funniest thing, possibly the most ironical, is that, for the first time in years, I have the sensation the apartment is bursting with love, albeit a sad love. When we emerge on to the landing, the widow from the apartment across the hall opens her door. At first, she eyes me with contempt, but she soon calms down when she realizes I look back at her with tenderness, melancholy even, as if I were sorry I wasn't going to see her again. The old woman stares at my wife and, having apparently understood she's in the presence of two people who no longer belong to this world, she bursts into tears with such despair she finally reveals the little girl she must once have been. Elena hugs her, kisses her on the forehead and says don't cry, little one. Having entered the elevator, we smile at her through the glass pane and don't utter a word until we reach the garage, where the car is ready to transport us to that destination nobody knows anything about. On emerging into the street, we look up, me toward our apartment, Elena toward the sky. I then drive toward one of the cliffs that surround this city. I observe the trees standing by the road. I like trees, I don't know why. I think my wife does as well because she looks relaxed and at one moment she places her hand on mine. In the rear-view mirror, I see the city receding. The street lamps go out as the sun appears on the horizon. The delivery vans go about their business. Lights go on in several windows. And I take for granted life will be exactly the same once we disappear round the bend on that cliff.

Only one acknowledgement:
To Carmen Tejedor,
for all the lives you've saved.

ABOUT THE AUTHOR

ÁLVARO COLOMER is a writer and a journalist. The novels *La calle de los suicidios* (The Street of Suicides), *Mimodrama de una ciudad muerta* (Mimedrama of a Dead City) and *Uppsala Woods* comprise a trilogy about death in the city, casting an outlook on the phenomenon of death and suicide in contemporary society from various points of view. He has also published the non-fiction books *Se alquila una mujer* (Woman For Hire) and *Guardianes de la memoria* (Guardians of Memory)—the first, a wide-ranging report about prostitution in Spain featuring short accounts based on true facts, and the second, a travel book dealing with five European locations marked by major historical events (Auschwitz, Chernobyl, Guernica, Transylvania and Lourdes) which was awarded the International Prize for Excellence in Journalism in 2007.

He has also co-written *El chico que vivía encerrado en una habitación* (The Boy who Lived Shut in a Room)—the first of three novels comprising the trilogy "Terror en la red" (Web Terror) to be published throughout 2013—and taken part in several anthologies.

He contributes to newspapers *El Mundo* and, occasionally, *Der Tagesspiegel*, as well as other Spanish media such as *La Vanguardia* (http://blogs.lavanguardia.es/el-arquero), *Yo Dona, Cultura/s, Qué Leer, Mercurio* or *Primera Línea*.

ABOUT THE TRANSLATOR

JONATHAN DUNNE translates from the Bulgarian, Catalan, Galician and Spanish languages. He has translated work by Tsvetanka Elenkova, Alicia Giménez-Bartlett, Lois Pereiro, Carme Riera, Manuel Rivas and Enrique Vila-Matas among others. He has edited and translated a two-volume *Anthology of Galician Literature 1196-1981 / 1981-2011* for the Galician publishers Edicións Xerais and Editorial Galaxia and a supplement of *Contemporary Galician Poets* for the UK magazine *Poetry Review*. He has written two books about language and translation—*The DNA of the English Language* and *The Life of a Translator*—as well as the poetry collection *Even Though That*. He directs the publishing house Small Stations Press.